When the Past meets the Present...

◆

When the Past meets the Present...

...then, there is no future!

◆

Written by a 14-year-old author!
JOHN ORIZON

Writers Club Press
San Jose New York Lincoln Shanghai

When the Past meets the Present...
...then, there is no future!

Writers Club Press
an imprint of iUniverse.com, Inc.

For information address:
iUniverse.com, Inc.
5220 S 16th, Ste. 200
Lincoln, NE 68512
www.iuniverse.com

ISBN: 0-595-14305-9

Printed in the United States of America

Acknowledgements

I would like to thank: my family and most of all my mother for her support and "funding," my brothers, Agnes Katsianos school for bringing the English version to perfection, Marg Gilks, Nancy Goldenberg, Marilyn & Tom Ross for their ideas, the people of IUniverse and IUniverse itself, George Zografos, Hellen Alafodimou and everybody else who worked hard and believed in my ideas and dreams. I would also like to say "thank you" to that "somebody," man or woman, I didn't remember to include in this list!

Introduction

Like tears of wind, the wave on the rocks
Ports, rivers it hasn't counted
Merely the stars, the ones here, the ones farther
The mind will ask only for those
And the rock will glare, the wheel, the pump
Wings to fly, it doesn't have, it will invent!

The deeds of his, mast of the world
And he, steering wheel to loves and hatreds

Great powers, responsibility of a hatchling
Sails that ravel, scraped by labor
And struggle, finishing at another struggle
For a land…
For an end…

Here is the land, but where is the port?
Works of men, their mistakes
Work of those and people's journey
Against the wind, by the wave…

Scream of a child, verses of his
Pages of history!

...then the legs bent
they didn't stand the weight
and...
like a wind that constantly blows
like a sun that rises
like the star that stands up there
like the dream that ceases breathing
no one felt sorry for it
no one said what a pity
a love seized it
and it was lost in the wave...

Tears like ink, sea is your paper
How come your glare is painting dark?

THE SIGNS...

You never heard it coming.
And like a setting sun...
you saw it but you didn't speak!

BUENOS AIRES
DECEMBER 21, 1997
CNN

"Two deaths occurred today at Buenos Aires, local time 01.20 and 02.10 respectively. The police reported that the suspected murder victims, two women, were discovered at a park and at the seashore.

It was really gruesome. Her hands were covered in scratches. You had to have been there. They looked more like scraps...you know."

"These were the words, spoken off the record, of the young man at the medical-"

The burly man raised a hand and pressed the off button on the television. He blocked the screen with his body. "I'm fed up, listening to such nonsense," he said and turned his head towards his wife. "Do you believe that?"

"Everybody is innocent until proven otherwise," she muttered.

Her husband's attitude changed. "Can I ask you something? Why do you always mix your business with home? Okay, you're a lawyer, a good lawyer, but learn at last to discriminate. What else could do such things, what else could treat a human like that, other than a...an animal?"

She looked at him strangely. "Man is also an animal..."

"Yes, yes I know. Man is also an animal. You will soon say that the young man was lying."

"You can't know that, either," she muttered again, looking at the painting above the sofa. It was a beautiful painting, and well-crafted. It radiated serenity and calmness. That was how she would like to feel her-self, during these moments. No talk, no fuss, only a spark in the dark-ness. A spark to give her courage, to soften the loneliness that sometimes is so beautiful. That loneliness was what her husband wanted to destroy now.

"I'm going to bed; I don't want to talk anymore with you. I don't know how you manage it, but you always get on my nerves."

"Goodnight," she said. Of course, she received no response.

She heard twelve footsteps on the timeworn wooden staircase. The absolute quietness didn't give her any other option but to notice them. She counted twelve, and surely there were twelve, but why all this worry?

The woman felt her face turn pale. Her eyes looked straight ahead and her hands fluttered on the arms of the chair. In all that unjustified upset, her mind managed to convince her. The staircase had fourteen stairs; why were only twelve footsteps heard? She immediately sought a logical solution: was there a carpet on two of the stairs? Did he take two stairs in one step? But no, it wasn't just that.

The woman's intuition, that unique instinct, was telling her something. There was something here, in the house with them, near to them, something that definitely didn't wish their well-being. Her mind seemed to have stopped, she didn't know what she should do; she caught herself feeling very frightened. Her ego persuaded her to find the courage to finally go up there. To see what was there, to see if her husband was all right.

She rose from her seat soundlessly, and walked slowly, like a cat stalk-ing its prey, only this time the prey was in a different environment and had a different character. She headed towards the staircase. Took a deep breath and went on. The sounds from the creaking old wood seemed too loud to her. The heel of her right shoe thumped. "I should have taken them off," she thought. "Damn the moment I agreed to go to that reception, my husband-"

Suddenly she stopped, stunned.

If she had her glasses she would be even more certain, but without them she could still make out someone lying on the floor. If she went on a little more, if she climbed a few more stairs, she would know with certainty what had happened.

Dreadful thoughts flooded her mind. A sound interrupted her thoughts. Something dripped, up there. "It might be the tap," she thought, but she wasn't sure. Doubts followed one another. She heard the sound a second time, then a third, and a fourth. The fifth time, she didn't just hear but also saw a drop falling on the stair in front of her. It was red and looked like...blood.

She froze. She didn't even move her eyes. She stood there, in that position, staring at that liquid trickling from stair to stair.

The dripping sounds were followed by another sound.

She was covered in sweat by now. Panicked as she was, she didn't wonder anymore. She turned and started running down the stairs. And then she heard a shrill sound, a twitter, louder than the dripping sounds. She didn't want to know what it was, and kept running.

She would feel safe only if she managed to get outside. Doors opened one after another. Only ten feet left to go. She grabbed the door handle and at the same moment heard a knock. It came from the drawing room, the room where the staircase was, but not just from there.

She didn't think any longer, but simply turned the handle. It was locked; her panic didn't let her see the keys in the keyhole at first. She unlocked the door hurriedly and opened it.

She heard footsteps behind her, footsteps coming faster and faster.

She surged outside, moving with all the strength that was left in her. She tripped, rolled twice, gained her feet and started running. She heard the door creak as it opened wider and wished she had closed it behind her. Thirty feet ahead, she saw another house-their neighbors; she knew them. They would open to her, even though it was midnight.

She reached their door and rang the doorbell three times. She heard a knock behind her. It sounded like it was coming from far away. She heard a second knock, much louder than the first. The animal must be close behind her by now.

She started pounding on the door.

The door opened, revealing a man standing behind it. The woman rushed into the house, screaming helplessly, knocking the man down. She heard a third knock. She ran up the stairs she found in front of her.

The predator followed her, ignoring the man, who saw nothing but a shadow-a dark figure that passed rapidly in front of him.

She ended up at a window. Looking down, she saw a mound of garbage. Without a second thought, she jumped...

She must have been knocked unconscious for a few seconds. She noticed she still lay between black ragbags. She raised her head, by now covered with scratches and bruises, as if she had suffered the whole world's misery.

In front of her, she could only make out a grayish mist; it had legs like a fowl and the leathery skin of a reptile. Its eyes glowed a yellowish color. They stared at her like a hunter who faces its prey. It was then that she realized her life was over.

The apple of its eye got up, looking observant, hostile. The predator bent its head and lifted its tail. It attacked.

She didn't even have time to understand, to scream, to feel regret for what followed.

Two days later

"What do you believe about all this?" a policeman asked his partner.

He was slow to answer. He didn't seem to have heard the question. He was looking dazedly the at dead woman being dragged out of the garbage mound. The stretcher waited a little farther away to take the mutilated, blood-covered remains of her body to the morgue.

"You've never seen a corpse before, have you?" the first policeman asked again, trying to dispel his partner's frightened attitude. "Here, you'll probably have to get used to it," he added. "We had three more victims last night."

His partner turned towards him. "All alike, I suppose."

"Not exactly. This victim looks as if it has been eaten, the rest don't. However, I must admit they resemble each other!"

He looked at him strangely. "How did you come to that conclusion?" he asked.

"I don't know, call it 'police genius'," the first policeman said, and laughed.

It was obvious that the other wasn't listening. His eyes were constantly turned towards their sergeant, in the phone booth nearby. He saw the sergeant nodding. He seeming troubled. He put the phone down and headed towards his car.

"You know, it's not just the police genius" the first policeman added. The other one turned and faced him.

"What genius?"

"I mean...consider that, in both cases, the victim died in front of witnesses."

"I don't get what you mean."

"Whatever killed her had certainly picked her out from the beginning. It ignored the rest of the people around her and attacked only her, the one it had picked out from the beginning."

"So, how do we know it's not human?"

"No, I don't mean that. Why don't you tell me what animal picks its victim out of a herd and attacks that one only?"

"I don't know, maybe lions could do that. When a member of the pride kills an animal, the rest gather around the kill, ignoring the animals that take flight."

"These two are different cases, if you think about it, although it could be so," the first policeman answered, growing nervous.

"Why bother? This isn't our job." He didn't seem to be listening; he was wrapped up in his thoughts.

"Hey captain, are you still here?" the first policeman prompted.

"It's too clever for an animal," his partner muttered.

"What did you say?"

"Three women and one man; it attacks systematically, and the damned thing is aware of their weaknesses."

"I can't hear what you're saying," the policeman's colleague said.

"That might be better," he said to himself.

"That might be better!"

NEW YORK
FEBRUARY 4, 1998
NEWSPAPER ARTICLE

"...her face was pale. The only life signs were some convulsions that grew more and more frequent. Her eyes were so dark that you really wondered if she could see or not, if she was alive or dead. The only thing certain was that it wouldn't be long before she was gone. She had only a few moments left.

The medics carrying the stretcher moved quickly, but even so, they knew their attempts were in vain. One of them nearly fell; maybe because he had to hold the bag of serum high; maybe not. The eyes of the people gathered around were also dark, but theirs had something hers were deprived of-life.

The ambulance door closed behind the stretcher and everyone realized that when it opened again, it wouldn't return what had been so unjustly taken.

She isn't the only one, however. Twelve more people have fallen victim to this terrible virus. Scientists say it's a new, faster AIDS, and nobody argues.

A few other magazines like ours support the so-called "judges opinion"-that New York should be under quarantine, something virtually impossible. It's also been said that this opinion was expressed by the president of the United States.

The opinion of our magazine will remain neutral. We will not support any of the opinions stated so far. And that is because this time, we're not talking about an actor's private life, but about the lives in an entire city."

-by Dennis Harvey

FEBRUARY 6, 1998
DAILY NEWSPAPER TITLES

1-NeoGene the new Savior
2-The human victory
3-NeoGene made its best
4-Man against nature
5-A company with human feelings
6-A serum has saved the earth

1-NeoGene the new Savior

Nobody else has died as a result of the epidemic that spread through New York three days ago, when thirteen people were identified as carriers of the new virus. Their deaths were painful, cruel and unfortunately, very quick. Had they lived longer, they may have benefited from the new achievement of NeoGene, VG-35. This new oral vaccine was given free to all the stricken-approximately two hundred people within four hours-and it is still dispensed for free at all drugstores without a prescription. The production of the drug is of course limited exclusively to the company that invented it. NeoGene itself has offered enormous amounts of the vaccine to the city hospitals. Authorization to use the drug without a doctor's prescription was given by hospitals too, for the sake of faster and more immediate effects.

The Secretary of State characteristically declared that he isn't used to such generosity. Surely commercial profit was hidden behind those good deeds...

However, people don't listen to such cautions. The only thing they know is that mankind managed to remedy a disaster of its own creation. NeoGene managed to perfect and produce an oral vaccine that would normally have taken weeks to develop, and, according to the public, simply saved thousands, maybe millions, of people!

-by Paula Randolph

4-Man against nature

Life nowadays is a constant struggle between man and nature. Undoubtedly, nature gave birth to man, but who managed to subdue the other? The answer was given today at daybreak with the invention of a new antiviral drug, which not only saves mankind but also commands nature's weapons. The question arising at this point is, who created this strain of virus? Definitely humans, you'd say; with nature's interference, I would add. There wouldn't be any virus at all if nature hadn't created one in the first place. However, biology always provides a solution to every problem. I'm sure all of you remember the day when an effective treatment for AIDS was announced. The only thing man had to do was to turn nature's own weapons against it...

-by Roxana Nelson

5-A company with human feelings

It's really amazing how a multinational company can manage to act so humanely. It is obvious that this company's policy is directed at the need for salvation rather than profit. This company understood public feeling and decided to do what the other biotechnological companies had avoided for so long.

Despite financial difficulty and stocks off half a point, the company continues to execute a universal program for saving New York, America and the whole planet.

-by Urania Sumner

SIDNEY
NOVEMBER 29, 1999

A dewdrop trickled down the leaf of a palm tree and dropped to the mud, making a small circle on the ground. The rain, one of the notorious sudden rainstorms of Australia, had left its mark on Sidney this night. Two people were reported dead.

"The car must have skidded on the slippery road surface," a passerby said.

The scene was frightful. The tree the car had struck was almost destroyed; the trunk was broken in half. A mass of crumpled sheet-metal completed the scene-the car that had crushed itself against the bent tree. Not far away, a red puddle gradually swelled in the rain. The ambulance sped for the hospital, its siren shattering the monotonous sound of the running water.

The Sidney police remained at the scene to guard the lifeless, broken pieces. The truth was that the rain wasn't enough to justify the accident. Maybe the driver was drunk, something the autopsy would turn up in a couple of hours. Or it could simply be a case of carelessness. If so, they wouldn't pursue any investigation before dawn.

"What's worse that could happen to me today?" one of the policemen asked, looking at the car. "Here we are, two cops alone outside a park, looking at each other."

"They'll be back in an hour Jimmy; it's no big deal."

"Yeah, right! Nothing much happened today; I can see you like sitting here with wet shoes and a soaked uniform. What else can we expect?"

Barry gave him an odd look, took a cigarette out of his pocket, and put it in his mouth.

"Do you need a light?" Jimmy asked him.

"Turn it off, okay?" Barry said shortly, glaring at him while he held the cigarette in his hand.

Jim laughed. "Calm down, I was just being polite…" he stopped talking because he noticed Barry's nervousness. "He's always nervous," Jim thought. "He doesn't talk much; he keeps what's bothering him inside. He always says things he doesn't mean." Same thing now. He sat silently under the eucalyptus, which was dripping every now and then, and kept the cigarette between his lips, without lighting it. Many people recognized him merely from that habit. Jim knew more about him, because they had been friends since early childhood.

The darkness became even more threatening as a cloud covered the moon, depriving them of its valuable light. Barry lifted his eyes to look at the sky.

"Are you afraid?" Jim asked in the absolute stillness.

Barry frowned at him. "What?" he said, as if he had never heard the word "afraid" before.

"I am not hiding it," Jim added. "I'm afraid."

"Why do you say that?"

"I don't know. How about you?"

Barry didn't answer right away. Something inside him was telling him not to answer. He felt the fear; he felt what he had forgotten since he was a little kid. Neither of them moved.

Jim, remaining still, turned only his eyes towards the car.

"Can you see it?" he asked.

Barry turned his eyes towards the car too. "Not well," he answered. "Damned darkness, I…"

He stopped talking. A black figure was standing still in front of him.

Barry felt his heart beating fast. He could clearly see the figure's head, while the rest of its body was enveloped in the darkness, as if it was one with the night. "I can see it now," he whispered, barely moving his lips.

Jim wasn't listening. He just kept looking ahead, frozen in his place. And that was because he had realized something Barry hadn't noticed till then. The animal had turned its head towards them; it stared at them without moving at all. That could mean two things. It was either scared of them, or it was preparing to attack.

Lightning flashed high in the sky, briefly, but long enough for them to see the creature's feral yellow eyes and scaly gray skin. The two men didn't move at all. Their faces were covered in cold sweat. Their breathing came deeper, faster.

The lightning flashed again. But this time, there was nothing there. The animal was no longer in front of them, but it could be nearby, even next to them, or behind them. That realization startled them.

"The moment I stand up, follow me," Barry whispered without turning his head to look at Jim. He swallowed with difficulty, then managed to stammer, "To the police car."

It started raining. Barry wanted to cross himself but he knew he shouldn't. The only thing he wished at that moment was to stay alive, and in order to do that, he had to get out of this damned place immediately. If he stayed any longer he would end up a victim of that animal, which he'd seen now for the first time, but felt like he had known since he was born.

He heard a sound behind him. Startled, he started running fast, and didn't stop. Jim followed. Neither of them looked back. They kept their eyes straight ahead, on the police car.

The car was only a short distance away, but the predator was fast. Both men heard its footfalls closer and closer behind them.

Barry reached the car; he opened the door and threw himself into the driver's seat and slammed the door shut behind him. Only then did he have time to wonder where Jim was. He peered through the window.

Jim was only a few feet from the car, but it didn't matter anymore. The animal leaned over Jim's blood-covered body, mouth open, looking at its victim. Jim raised his head out of the mud for the last time. Barry saw his eyes…they were full of wonder and sorrow. Jim stretched his hand out, trying to move forward. The animal let him crawl for a while, then grabbed him again. It leaped on the man with both its legs and hooked claws into his shoulders. It bent forward, and using one wicked claw, it cut the policeman's back open in a straight line, tearing him in half. Jim's hand dropped into the muddy water.

Barry had stopped looking. He couldn't think. He didn't even want to know what that beast was. His disgust turned to grief for his dead friend, and he leaned on the steering wheel and started crying.

As he wept, a wave of hatred ran through his mind. Without thinking, without even looking outside, he threw open the door and rushed out.

The animal raised its head and watched Barry as though daring him to do something. Barry lowered his hand to his pistol and drew it from the holster. He quickly pointed the gun at the creature's head.

The animal glared at the gun. It opened its jaws, showing its teeth threateningly. A horrible sound came from its mouth.

Barry fired the gun three times.

Blood splattered the policeman's face as parts of the animal were blown away. The creature started screeching loudly, its body writhing in the puddles formed by the rain. Barry watched it convulse for five seconds before he unloaded his gun into its gray flesh.

The animal stopped moving. Its tail lifted, then dropped, quivering, after a while.

Barry walked around the animal, then dropped on his knees.

Two sirens were heard, coming closer.

The regular beep of the electrocardiograph told the policeman he was still alive. Barry opened his eyes hesitantly, shielding them with his hand. It was morning; he must have slept for at least five hours. Despite pressure from the police department, the doctors hadn't allowed anyone to wake him up. He'd needed to rest.

Barry's first impression was of a white haze that slowly solidified into the ceiling of a room. He turned his head and saw a small bed table, and next to that, two small closets. He realized he was at a hospital.

He took a deep breath, then another, and looked around; there was no one in the room. He closed his eyes again and tried to remember what had happened.

He heard a door open and opened his eyes. Accompanied by a nurse, two men, formally dressed, entered the room. One of them sat down next to Barry's bed, while the other remained standing, absently studying a tray of surgical instruments. He took a cigar out of his pocket.

"Excuse me, you're not allowed to smoke in here," the nurse said, then added, "Don't get him too tired."

"Don't worry," the man replied, and put the cigar back in his pocket. The nurse glanced at Barry, then left, closing the door behind her.

Barry looked at the man sitting next to him.

"Policemen…right?" he said in a low, weak voice.

Both men ignored his question.

"Did you see it too?" Barry asked.

The two men looked each other. After a while they turned towards Barry's bed again. "What are you talking about?" one of them asked.

Barry's eyelids lowered. If they were policemen, they were supposed to be informed about the case. "Are you cops, or am I wrong?" he asked, and sat up, leaning on the pillow.

"Listen, pal," one of the two men said, taking a cigar out off his pocket again, "we don't know anything, but listen to this: you don't know either. You have amnesia; you don't remember anything."

Barry looked at him, confused. He looked at the cigar. "Those cigars should be too expensive for you, mister policeman. I suppose you forgot you're not allowed to smoke in here. It's bad for my health."

"I'm sure you heard what I said clearly, and I won't repeat it." The man took four steps to the door, opened it and told his colleague to follow him. Just before he left, he looked back at the injured man.

"Take your last comment as personal advice," he said. "If you really care about your health, you'd better listen to us."

" I listened to you, all right, but I can't assure you I'll keep listening,'" Barry said as the door slammed so forcibly that he was unsure whether his words had reached their ears.

5 hours later

He could see his house through the window of the car. It felt like days since he'd last left the place, even though not even a day had passed. That brief time had been full of nightmares and all those things that make life seem harder and longer.

He pulled some money out of his pocket and paid the cab driver, told him to keep the change, and then walked quickly towards the house. It was not just longing that made him hurry to touch the door, but also fear. It made him see his house as shelter.

Barry put his keys in the keyhole and unlocked the door, then opened it and left them in the door. He dropped heavily onto the couch, sending up a cloud of white dust. He found the television remote control and meticulously searched the channels, ending up at a newscast on a local channel.

The newscaster described an animal attack the previous night, and reported that the victims...

The newscaster's words vaguely troubled Barry. He suddenly realized what bothered him: the last word the newscaster had used. It didn't take long to understand why. He was alive; there weren't two victims but one-Jim. At that moment, Barry heard the newscaster adding that two men's bodies had been transferred during the night.

Barry, upset, grabbed the remote control again and increased the volume. He had to hear his name to be certain. When he did, he didn't move at all.

"I'm dead," he whispered. "Everybody thinks I'm dead." He struggled to grasp what was going on.

He quickly rose from the couch and stood for a while, listening carefully. Then he rushed to the door but-bad luck!-it was locked. He'd left the keys in the lock on the other side, he suddenly remembered. Somebody had taken advantage of his carelessness, trapping him in his own house.

When he realized what was happening, he ran full-tilt toward the window and jumped through, breaking the glass. He landed on a bush.

There was a deafening explosion behind him.

747

Because sunset is always whispering.
And you, you could never hear whispers

WHEN THE REAL STORY BEGINS
AND HUMANITY ENDS
2004

"In conclusion, I'd like to remind all of you what this day means to the United States and especially to you here in Washington, where you felt the breath of the virus that broke out in New York six years ago. You were informed immediately; nothing was kept from you, the people and spirit of America. We took responsibility for this decision back then, and we will accept this position again tomorrow!"

The people below started cheering so loudly that they drowned out the sound from the speakers. Clive, the president of the United States, left the podium, got into his luxurious car and was taken to the White House.

Reporters filled the entrance, all doing their best to get a quote or even a couple of words from that important man. The gate opened and policemen created a ringer in front of it, blocking the people out. Clive got out of his car and walked hurriedly, without looking back. He reached the entrance and only then turned and waved at the crowd of television reporters and cameramen outside the gate. The gate closed behind him, disappointing the reporters.

The corridors of the White House that the president walked down no longer left him with a sense of glamour. He headed to a conference room where eleven people waited around a round table made from costly exotic woods.. Nervous, Clive walked to an empty seat and sat down. He immediately noticed the worried silence permeating the room.

"Maybe now you can tell me what's going on," Clive said. "Right, Mr. Foster. What's all this fuss about? Has it ever occurred to you that I don't like to be interrupted in the middle of a speech? This had better be urgent."

"Mr. President, please calm down. We didn't call you here for nothing."

"I certainly hope not!"

"I'm sure your feelings will change," Foster said, "when you hear what we have to tell you."

"What's going on?" the president demanded.

Nobody dared to speak. Clive looked closely at Foster. "You'll give me that answer," he said.

Foster swallowed with difficulty and glanced at the colleagues on his right and left, who lowered their eyes to stare at the table. Now the urgency seemed much more real than before.

"What we're trying to say, Mr. President," Foster said in a hesitant voice, "is that an airplane is flying out of control at this moment."

Clive rolled up his sleeves; everybody around the table took a deep breath.

"The bad thing is…"

"Go on, God damn it, go on!"

"It's a passenger plane, Clive, full of many innocent people…"

Clive's face froze. "Jesus Christ," he managed to mumble. "What happened up there?"

It was some time before anyone spoke.

"We don't know," Foster finally said. "There's no communication at all."

"What do we do now?" the man sitting opposite the president asked, breaking the silence. "Minutes are valuable; we can't afford to lose any time."

"You're right," Clive said and stood up. "Initiate emergency procedures. Make sure everybody is informed."

"Whatever you think," Foster said, signaling the rest to implement the president's wishes immediately.

The committee members scattered, hurrying off in different directions. An air of near-panic permeated the White House.

Foster approached the president amidst all the fuss. "Clive, I'd like to ask you something."

"Say it quickly, I'm busy."

"The elections aren't very far away and-"

"Foster, when I heard about the plane, a thousand thoughts went through my mind in a second!"

"So what?"

"I'm telling you that the elections weren't one of them," he said and Foster looked embarrassed. "The safety of the passengers on that plane was my first thought and the one that froze me for a whole minute!" the president added.

Foster smiled slyly. "And how about the spirit of America?"

"What did you say?"

"What I'm saying is, will we inform the citizens?"

"I think this is something they should know!"

"Well, that's all I wanted to know" Foster said, and headed towards the exit. In a while the whole world would know what was happening a few miles above their heads…or at least they would think so…

THE FIRST COUNCIL

"Mr. President, you're being called to the council being held now."

"I know, tell them I'm coming."

"It's urgent, sir," the officer added. The president looked at him, annoyed. "At least, that's what they told me to tell you," the officer said. He finally convinced the president to follow him to the conference room.

The officer opened the door and white light from the hallway spilled into the conference room. "The president has arrived," the officer announced.

"Have a seat, Mr. President," said the Secretary of Defense, who was standing next to a hologram base that took on color again when the door closed. "I will repeat the previous comments so that you can hear them too."

A three-dimensional image of an airplane, viewed at ground level, formed on the hologram base. The plane, an older type, had not been replaced when Boeing introduced a series of new jumbo jets. The president himself had rejected the replacement program. This fact, along with the upcoming election, put Clive in a very uncomfortable position.

"As I said earlier, we won't attempt to get the passengers out of the aircraft; that would be impossible. Our goal is to restore the plane to its original course and land it at the nearest airport."

"Which one in particular?"

"The 747 was on a Hong Kong-Paris-New York route. Somewhere in the middle of the second leg, it diverged from its course."

"It's over the Atlantic Ocean," Clive murmured, almost to himself.

"It's very possible that the plane will fly over Toronto." The members of the advisory committee looked at each other. In such a case, the Canadian government would consider them responsible for any repercussions if the airplane crashed.

"How far can the plane go on its existing fuel?"

"I suppose as far as Toronto, maybe a bit farther. Some of my assistants are working on that possibility now."

The door opened once more. The light spilling into the darkened room blinded the president, forcing him to shield his eyes.

Beneath his raised hand, he saw several people walk past the Secretary of Defense next to the hologram. Then the image changed, revealing a map that displayed the plane's current course. Clive, eyes still on the image, pulled his glasses from his pocket.

"The Boeing 747 is following, as you probably already know, the route from Paris to New York," one of the men who had just entered the room said. "There was no trouble from Hong Kong to Paris. This is its exact course, recorded by two of our satellites." He pointed to a red line. "Note also this white line, which was the plane's plotted course." He turned and entered some numbers on the keyboard to the right of the image.

The president frowned. The map showed that the plane had diverted from its course immediately after passing over the Azores. He didn't know why, but that fact made him shudder.

"From that point on," the young speaker said, "the plane diverted from its course to the present one, and at the same moment we lost communications. Whatever happened, it happened very quickly."

"I'm sorry to interrupt," someone from the back of the room said, "but it's necessary that I find out both the plane's current altitude and when it will enter American airspace."

The young speaker glanced at the president, who nodded consent.

"It's flying at 20,000 feet, sir...and it will be in U.S. airspace in approximately one hour and fifty-four minutes."

"Thank you very much," the advisor said and sat down again. He took a mobile phone out of his jacket and held it to his ear, muttering, "I hope I'm not bothering anyone."

"Any more questions?"

"Yes," said the vice-president as he stood up. He was a vigorous, clever person, who would make an ideal president, himself. "I've just listened all this time to things that don't do anything to help the situation. Above all, we must determine what we can do, and you must tell us what we can't do."

"I'm sorry, I thought you had been informed," the speaker said, perplexed. "It's a true miracle the plane is still in the air. So far, only the satellites have been able to locate it. Someone has destroyed all the communications systems-someone very clever!"

"Or lucky," Clive added.

"Tell me this," Foster said, "are we talking about a hijack?"

"No, I don't think so. The hijackers would have communicated with us, and if not, they would have a specific course, not this random one being tracked on our map. They would direct the plane where they wanted, making a turn first and then holding to a straight course. Don't forget that the deviations from the course we see definitely indicate an unstable environment, which would require those on board to remain constantly alert. Would hijackers have time to constantly check their course while watching for a possible conspiracy by the plane's displaced crew?"

"What if they're trying to make us think exactly that?" the vice-president suggested. "What if we're the suckers now?"

"Wait a minute," Clive interrupted. "We don't even know what happened on that plane, so it's better to avoid such speculation." The rest of the advisors murmured immediate agreement. "Time is against us right now," Clive added. "The Secretary of Defense has suggested a plan to me, which we will follow. He will describe it now; anyone having objections should speak right after. And something more: if the lives of the plane's passengers are eventually lost, I will consider myself responsible and I will tender my resignation." His announcement caused a stir and murmurs of respect from those present.

Just before the Secretary of Defense moved to the rostrum to announce the plan, someone voiced a last question.

"Excuse me but…how many people are on the plane?"

Everyone looked at the young speaker. He sighed. "Approximately four hundred and fifty people," he said. "Four hundred and fifty."

MISSION IMPOSSIBLE!

The Secretary of Defense looked at his watch. It showed exactly 21.30. Three-quarters of an hour had already passed since they'd been informed of this terrible incident. The plane was just over an hour away from entry into U.S. airspace. The handpicked men who would undertake the mission knew that. Why, then, were they so late?

Car headlights appeared in the darkness. A military jeep had entered the airport and now headed towards the Secretary of Defense. It turned suddenly and stopped in front of him, and one, two, four hardy soldiers jumped from it, prepared for the worst.

"You know what you have to do," he said. "The lives of four hundred and fifty people are in your hands. That means that each of you must save about one hundred-" The Secretary of Defense stopped speaking as a fifth soldier jumped out of the jeep. If you could call that a jump. He carried a stack of books.

"He's the technician, and a pilot for the 747, as well. His participation was decided to be definitely necessary," one of the officials standing next to the Secretary of Defense said. Then he leaned close to the Secretarys' ear to whisper, "No one else volunteered."

"At your orders, sir, or whatever you say around here," the pilot said, laughing.

"Around here," the Secretary said sternly, "we make sure we don't ramble." The pilot cleared his throat nervously, realizing that neither the people nor the situation were appropriate for jokes. "So, what are you waiting for? Get on board," the he added, pointing at an aircraft whose battered fuselage indicated that this was a very old, worn machine.

Only one word, picked out in black lettering, could be made out through the dirt on the plane's surface. Anyone with no knowledge of aircraft would never realize that word was *Harrier*. In fact, this was a descendant of the original Harriers. It was a specially-modified aircraft, with a compartment mounted beneath it that allowed crew to be transferred between airplanes in mid-air.

The five soldiers, or more properly, the four soldiers and the technician-pilot, boarded the aircraft. The Defense Secretary and those accompanying him got into a shiny BMW and drove away.

Those on board took their places. Allan, the naïve pilot, left his books on the floor and took a seat where he could watch the two men operating the military aircraft.

Ever since he'd been little, he'd wanted to fly a military aircraft. Unfortunately, circumstances had allowed him only training for piloting passenger airplanes. He had dreamt of other things for himself. Maybe this was his big chance; maybe if he managed to save the 747, his dreams would come true. He could become somebody.

A tremendous shake interrupted his thoughts. The aircraft heaved vertically, causing a deafening hum. The jet engine nozzles finally swung horizontal and the aircraft shot forward, towards the unknown, taking crew and five souls along with it-five sparks of hope that it would never bring back again...

Clive watched the courses of the two airplanes on an enormous screen. Around him, many people came and went, each with their own problems, but all of them related to the same issue. In all that fuss, Clive still heard a door open. He turned toward the sound and saw the Secretary of Defense dash into the room and fix his eyes on the gigantic screen.

"How far are the two airplanes from each other?" the Secretary asked.

"The transport aircraft will take at least ten more minutes to reach the 747," a young man working nearby answered. The Secretary, however, seemed not to have heard him. He and Clive stood next to each other and watched the two spots indicating the planes wink on the screen. Who could imagine that, the moment that red light winked off, the lives of four hundred and fifty people would simultaneously cease to exist!

"Mr. President," someone said, "we received a passenger list from Paris. According to that, 123 American citizens boarded the plane in Hong Kong; one of them got off in Paris, while eighty-two more boarded."

"It's February," Clive said to himself. "Many people travel now because of the slow period businesses experience after Christmas."

A device suddenly transmitted a communication signal.

"It's from the transport aircraft," the young man operating the radio said.

"Put me through," the Defense Secretary said, and picked up the phone in front of him.

"...do you copy, I repeat, do you copy?"

"This is the Secretary of Defense."

"I'm proceeding with the operation, code name 'Rising Sun.'"

"You have my permission to proceed," the Secretary said and laid his finger on a fingerprint detector.

"I ask for verification from the President."

The Secretary looked at Clive. He didn't answer immediately.

"This is Bennett Clive," he said, and laid his finger on the detector as well. "Do what you have to; proceed with our plan."

"Yes sir," were the last words heard from the radio. Then it was turned off.

They were only fifty feet away from the passenger plane's tail. Tension ran high in the Harrier. Allan crossed himself. The two soldiers sitting opposite him looked at each other and smiled ironically.

A sudden shake made Allan close his eyes. He was afraid, and he did-
n't deny to himself. The darkness behind his eyelids made him think of
his childhood. Back then, he would refuse to follow his friends on a daring mission! Unfortunately, not many things had changed since then.
This time, he was not just endangering his life for the sake of simple
egoism or bravado. He would do so to prove to himself: "you did something great-you're not just anyone!"

The course of the Harrier seemed steady. Allan dared to open his
eyes. He saw the two soldiers in front of him unbuckle their seatbelts
and stand up. He did the same. He looked out the front windscreen of
the cockpit. To his great surprise, he didn't see the 747 in front of them
anymore. "I must have kept my eyes closed quite long," he thought. A
second shake threw him down.

"Hurry up, guys; I can't hold it here much longer," one of the two
pilots said from the cockpit. One of the soldiers wordlessly opened a
trapdoor beneath his feet and climbed into the chamber below. The
three other soldiers followed him. Last of all went Allan, who almost
wrenched his leg.

"Everything's set," said one of the soldiers as he closed the trapdoor
over their heads. Allan, being uninformed of how they would enter the
plane, nearly panicked.

"It's logical not to understand what's going on," one of the soldiers
said. "This project is kept top secret by the government."

"No one knows about it, so no one expects it, right?"

"Right. It was designed to deal with very extreme hijacking cases.
Only this time, we don't know what we'll face. That's why you're here."

Suddenly the floor jolted. They all felt the metal walls shaking. They
heard a tremendous metallic crunch, as if an iron beam had snapped. After
that, the ceiling panels rattled, while the floor plates stabilized. Allan
realized what had happened. The chamber they stood in was now attached
to the passenger plane where the transport aircraft had left it. Allan didn't
know what to do. He moved to a corner and crouched down.

The soldiers told him to keep his eyes closed. He felt something burn him repeatedly, as though sparks hopped around the compartment. It was quite a while before he opened his eyes and saw the soldiers standing in a circle around a small screen. A long instrument, so thin as to be almost imperceptible, extended from the screen through a big hole in the floor, disappearing into the interior of the 747.

Allan immediately realized what they were trying to do. But, why was there wonder all over their faces, why all that worry?

"What's going on?" he asked; one of the soldiers signed to him to move closer. Allan stood and fixed his eyes on the small screen.

"Do you see those two still red spots? They're the heat the two men radiate."

"Then where are the rest of the people?"

"That's the problem. I don't want to imagine the worst. But that's not all."

"What else is going wrong?" Allan asked, full of terror.

"Well, the spots…it's not normal that humans radiate that much heat. It's possible, but a person would have to run ten times around a football field, first."

"Be quiet," another soldier said, the senior officer of the team. He raised his hand and pointed at two of the team members. They would be the first to go down into the airplane.

Allan didn't look down. He just dropped and landed clumsily. He got up unassisted and looked around, but didn't see anyone. He fought panic. He opened the first door he found and ran into someone. It was the officer.

"You finally found the courage," he said to Allan in a sardonic voice. Allan drew away from him without saying a word. "You'd better follow us," the other said, and moved ahead.

They were getting close to the main door that led to the flight deck. They all concentrated on their movements; even the faintest sound could reveal their position to an enemy.

In front of Allan, the soldier's strides grew longer and faster. His behavior certainly didn't remind Allan of a scared or cautious man until, all of a sudden, the soldier froze.

Allan and the soldier a few steps behind him also stopped. They tried to see what had alerted their captain, what had made him freeze. Allan noticed something trickle down the strong man's neck. Sweat, Allan realized after a moment.

Allan couldn't see the officer's face but, judging from his ears, the man had turned red. What could it be that scared him so much, Allan wondered. He had to find out.

He took a step forward. There was no reaction from the soldier. He moved a little closer. His forehead felt hot, like he was burning with fever. The sweat that broke on it seemed cool to him. He had to move a little closer in order to get next to the big soldier. He was only a step away from discovering why they had stopped. As he took that last step, he realized he had made a very big mistake.

Clive sat on a chair, nervously tapping his pen on the table. He was lost in thought. In particular, something no one had considered so far was troubling him.

If the airplane kept to its present course, without anyone controlling it, then it would definitely fly over America and crash somewhere in Canada, maybe even in a city. The casualties in such a case would double, maybe number even more. Clive imagined the Boeing 747 going through buildings, plowing over streets, smashing cars and destroying everything in its path. The Canadian government would consider the United States responsible.

On the other hand, no one would dare take all responsibility for the shooting down of a 747 with four hundred and fifty passengers on board, passengers still likely to be alive. The team sent to get the plane back on a steady course and land it at the nearest airport was the only way out of this situation.

At that moment, Clive remembered words he'd heard earlier: "it's a miracle that the airplane is still up in the air." He shuddered. How would the technician repair any damage in such a short time?

"Sir, we've just been informed that all five are inside," the officer said. "Two of the soldiers, along with the technician, are heading towards the flight deck while the others are searching the rest of the plane."

Clive didn't answer. He kept tapping his pen on the table and absently watching the screen. Then he abruptly stood up, letting his pen drop to the floor. Everybody stared at him.

"What's wrong, Clive?" the Secretary of Defense asked him.

He didn't answer immediately. Finally he said, "I was wondering. If our men overpower the hijackers-if they exist-couldn't we somehow connect two, three or as many transport aircraft as are necessary to keep the 747 in the air when the fuel runs out? Then we could land it at a big airport."

Silence prevailed. All eyes turned to the Secretary.

"It would be very difficult. The connections must be very strong and totally balanced. Add to this the fact that it will all have to be done in the air...impossible."

"But it's worth a try, isn't it?"

The Secretary sighed. "There is no such equipment available, Clive. It would take approximately three hours to create the necessary equipment."

On hearing this answer, the president closed his eyes. He wanted to scream, to hit himself; for a moment, he even considered resigning. What would this do to his career, if he couldn't handle such a huge responsibility?.

The pervading silence made the air in the 747 seem even stuffier.

When Allan saw the dead body, he thought of himself as completely stupid not only because he had stepped forward but also because he had agreed to undertake this mission. His ambitions had now turned against him.

He heard the officer next to him whisper, "I'm going back with the others. Whatever did this has returned to the seats at the back of the plane." He pointed at three bloody footprints. Allan was terrified that he may be left alone. "You will stay here with him and try to regain control of this damned plane," the officer said to the other soldier, offering a breath of relief to the scared pilot.

Allan moved towards the door to the flight deck with slow and careful steps. His hand froze before it touched the handle as he heard a chilling sound behind him. He stood still, wondering what had made the loud twitter. What kind of creatures were on that plane?

Several minutes passed and Allan heard no other strange sound. He felt stupid to have stayed still for so long. Now was the time for him to take action; to perform his duty.

He'd looked at the human body that he'd passed on his way to the door. A terrible realization smothered the disgust he had initially felt. The dead man's skin was growing livid around the wounds, while parts of the man's belly and his legs were gone. "Something must have bitten him," Allan thought, and his legs started shaking. If he ran, he could possibly save himself. If he stayed here, he was already dead.

With a sudden move, he twisted his body to one side and froze there, perplexed and wondering where the other soldier had gone.

His heart beat so fast that he believed it could be heard several feet away. He tried to come up with a logical excuse, some reasonable explanation. In his panic, he managed to convince himself that the other soldier had followed his colleague despite the order the other had given him. That thought encouraged Allan enough to take a careful, but inevitably noisy, step. The stress the situation produced pushed him into thoughtless actions that could cost his life.

Allan was fully aware of that, but for him, all that mattered anymore was that he had managed to get even closer to the door that stood between him and a second chance for life. He took two more steps-small, careful ones this time. Six feet in front of him was the door.

"The flight deck is just beyond that," he whispered, and immediately realized what a stupid thing he had just done!

The whisper was enough to call the thing that had killed the man behind the flight deck's door.

"Damn!" Clive shouted, drawing the attention of everybody working around him. "I can't make a decision on such a serious matter!"

"But you must, Mr. President," the Secretary of Defense insisted.

"Do you know what you're telling me right now? I'll tell you! You're asking me to deliberately kill four hundred and fifty people to prevent danger to others later, because nobody knows how we can save them. Which of all these solutions is the right one?"

"Excuse me, Mr. President," someone said from the back of the room. Clive turned towards the voice. "We've just received a notice from the United Nations, in New York. According to some information from LaGuardia airport in New York-"

"Just say what you want to say, sir ," Clive interrupted.

The employee looked sideways at him and lowered his eyes. "The airplane will reach our coast in eleven minutes."

Clive put his hand on his head and closed his eyes.

"If you wish to shoot it down, you must hurry. Don't take longer than ten and a half minutes."

The Defense Secretary pressed a button on his watch.

"You see, the plane's altitude is such that if you fire on it and don't entirely destroy it, parts of it will most likely fall along the U.S. coastline," the employee continued. "One more thing: it is now confirmed that the plane's fuel will run out over Toronto."

"Do we have any message from the crew of the transport aircraft?" the Secretary asked.

"No sir, absolutely nothing."

By now, everybody watched the president. He sat as if he was unable to move, holding his head in his hands.

He heard the Secretary saying, "Now it's your call, Clive," and stood up.

He didn't want to know why he was running, what the creature was that had frightened him so much. He went down the stairs he found in front of him in three jumps. Fear, the lust for life, made him uncharacteristically agile. The scream he heard from the floor above gave him the strength to continue. "They were all dead," he thought of the 747's flight crew.

Suddenly he beheld a horrible sight.

In front of him, people lay where they had fallen on the floor, their clothes red with the blood that flowed like a river between the bodies. Men, women, children-all were dead. Lifeless bodies lay on top of other bodies, their eyes wide open, full of terror.

And on top of all these bodies a strange, unearthly animal stared at him, perplexed.

"Velociraptor," his mind supplied. He didn't have time to wonder why. His every thought was frozen, along with his body.

The animal tilted its head and lifted its tail. Allan felt the last minutes like they lasted for ages. He closed his eyes and waited.

A human groan made him open them again. He saw the animal ripping off the raised hand of a man wriggling helplessly beneath it. Then the creature bent and, with a sudden move, tore a piece from the man's belly. The man convulsed before he passed away.

"He asked for help and he was offered death," Allan thought. He heard a knock behind him.

A second animal had landed behind Allan and was stealthily approaching him. The one in front of Allan, assessing the situation, ignored Allan.

That gave him another chance to fight before he died. Without hesitation, Allan ran straight ahead, heedless of where he would end up.

He barged into a door and instinctively rushed inside. He was in one of the washrooms. He shut the door behind him and locked it. When he turned away from the door, he came face to face with a blood-covered woman. She was still alive, but suffering unbearable pain.

Maybe he could relieve her pain.

"What happened in here?" Allan asked as he pulled her hand from her stomach. The wound was deep. There was no way she would survive.

"Wild animals," she gasped. "My child…wild animals." Allan struggled to make sense of what she said. "Attacked, all dead…my child…" the woman said for the last time. Allan hushed her, but then he realized she was not breathing.

He could hear the velociraptor's steps. He wanted to lie down and peek under the door, try to see where the hell that cold killer was. He wished he had a gun. Then he heard a second sound. The animal had opened the door of one of the washrooms across the aisle. Maybe the next one would be his. He heard a second door open.

"Now it's my turn," he thought, and shuddered.

The animal tried to open the door but it was locked. With a simple strike, it broke the lock and the handle dropped to the floor. It slowly pushed the door with its muzzle until it was wide open.

The animal leaned forward, smelling the woman's corpse in front of it. If it came in any further, it would see Allan, who was half-hidden under the woman's body. He listened carefully and eventually heard the animal leave.

"It's stupid," he thought with a wave of relief. He took several deep breaths to make up for those he had missed during the last few minutes. He'd been lucky twice, but that didn't necessarily mean there would be a third time.

Gently and slowly he pushed the dead woman's body from above him. He had gotten stiff in there, but that didn't bother him. He had to figure out what to do to save himself. He suddenly realized that there wasn't any escape. He was in a flying plane, something he had forgotten during the past few minutes. His life would end pretty soon, he knew. But strangely, it didn't matter to him anymore whether he lived or died. He had evaluated all that long ago, ten years ago, when he'd decided that "Yes, it's worth dying a hero!"

Now he felt much better. He had managed to find his real self, the one he had been looking for for a very long time. He'd always dreamt of being heroic, decisive, ready to die for anyone.

The last thing he had to do was to notify the government. He had to inform them of the situation up here, tell them that everyone was dead, even himself! Then they might have time to shoot the plane down over the ocean and avert any more tragic deaths. The only way he could accomplish that was to get the military team's radio. He remembered that the strongest man carried the radio, and that man was most likely dead. Minutes were valuable; he didn't ponder further. He stood up and, without caring if he made any noise, opened the door between him and those two bloodthirsty beasts.

He felt a deep cut to his back and heard the animal's twitter behind him. They'd been waiting for him! They had set a trap! They wouldn't stop him-this time, it wasn't just his own life that was at stake.

He ran through the dead people, passed over their lifeless bodies, keeping his eyes straight ahead. When he reached the stairs, he found the body of the muscular soldier. He bent and pulled at the radio but realized it was tied to the man's belt! With quick movements, he struggled to untie it. At the instant he freed the radio, he heard that knocking sound once more.

The animals were in front of him, watching his movements; they were playing with their last victim.

He started up the stairs one tread at a time, moving as fast as he could. He looked behind him and was terrified to see a velociraptor jumping them in threes! The moment he reached the top, he dashed in the flight deck, got inside and tried to close the door. The door jerked and knocked him down. When he got up, he faced the animal, which had tumbled onto the floor. He ran to the door and, with all the strength left in him, slammed it shut.

He fell down, breathing heavily and quickly. The sweat trickling down his neck had soaked his entire shirt. He took it off and held it to his forehead. He couldn't see well; he was dizzy. Despite the pain in his head, he heard a loud metallic sound coming from the door. The animal was trying to find its way in. It was hunting him!

The moment to reveal his decision had come. The president's decision would close this case either unpleasantly or pleasantly, if there was a choice. He would give everything precious he had-even his own life, his name!-to know what decision was the right one.

He took a deep breath and said clearly, "Let the plane keep flying." No one spoke. "We'll wait for further notice from the team on board." He sat down again.

A second, louder bang made the door buckle. It was only a matter of time before the creature tore it down. That gave Allan impetus to hurry.

He activated the radio and tried to contact the White House. Again the door sustained a blow and its metallic surface crumpled further. He didn't know how long it would hold. He placed his ear to the radio, hoping for a response.

"This is the White House. Report identification code."

"Listen," Allan said, "I don't have much time. Don't ask, just listen."

In Washington, silence prevailed in the room where the president sat.

"Everybody's dead, I repeat, everybody's dead, even me," Allan's voice said through the radio. "Shoot the plane down now that you've still got time."

"What's going on up there?" Clive shouted.

"Don't you understand what I'm telling you? Do it now, shoot-" A loud noise came from the speakers and the communication was cut off.

The Defense Secretary and the president looked at each other and reached an unspoken understanding.

"Give the order for launch now," the Secretary of Defense said to the young man sitting beside him. The young man looked at him incredulously and didn't move. "Why don't you do what I told you, damn it?" The young man didn't speak at all. He just raised his hand and showed his watch to Clive.

Time had run out.

ALLAN

He was lying in a corner without moving at all. The animal had stopped banging on the door. He had turned the radio off to give the impression to those on the ground that he was dead. He didn't want there any scruples to interfere when that launch button was pressed.

Everything would happen so fast.

He began recollecting his past. He retraced his childhood, his years in school, when all his schoolmates made fun of him because of his fears. He remembered his favorite toy, a little soldier that could speak and drive a remote-controlled chopper. He also remembered his mother and how she yelled at him every time he broke something. Then his mind moved over facts both sorrowful and scary. Facts that had occurred ten minutes ago.

That thought, however, unexpectedly woke an equally scary realization. He should have been dead by now. The plane should have been shot down. Terrified, he stood up and walked to the control board. He faced thousands of lights of various colors that shone through the windshield of the plane, with black sky behind. They weren't the lights of the control board. They were the lights of houses and cars, another world that pulsed with life, a life that was never appreciated enough by anyone.

This wasn't the first time he'd watched this sight. He had many hours of night flight, but this time was special. It was his last time.

He tried to figure out what had happened, why he was still midair. He assumed those in the White House hadn't believed him, but he couldn't be certain. He again lifted the radio and attempted to call them, but the device was dead. He had to find a way to crash the plane himself, if he could still pilot it. The only thing certain was that he couldn't soft-land it. Even if he managed to do so, the impact would probably kill him while freeing the raptors to kill more innocent people.

Even if the velociraptors were captured, destruction would simply be delayed a while. Human greed and curiosity would set them free again. Those unearthly figures should be exterminated and the cost of one more life seemed trivial in comparison to the advantage his death would gain.

Despite having a terrible headache, Allan tried to come up with a solution. He remembered that before the team boarded the 747, they had been informed what course the 747 would follow. He had the impression that it would fly over Toronto but would run out of fuel shortly afterward. The only opportunity he had was to take the plane down into Lake Ontario, but he would have to make corrections to the plane's course. He would die on impact, but the animals would drown in the plane.

But, would the airplane obey his commands from the cockpit, since everything in here was topsy-turvy? He paid attention to the condition of the cockpit, but now he could see it was a mess. The floor was spattered with blood spots around a straight stripe of blood. Cut wires hung from the ceiling, while the microphone at the pilot's seat dangled. The communication screen was dark. Something must have startled the animals, for them to go against the equipment like that. Maybe it was the flashing lights or the view of a world that was thousands of feet below them.

Allan checked to see if the autopilot was still working. He was disappointed. He opened a pocket in his trousers and took out a palmtop. If the control panel accepted any commands there was still hope.

The switches controlling the plane's course seemed hopelessly inaccessible. Allan made some calculations on his palmtop, which, according to the coordinates displayed of the plane's current position, gave the appropriate numbers for the change in the plane's course. Allan typed in the numbers and the palmtop showed that the change in course was successful. The 747 was heading towards that Great Lake, its final stop.

A strange sound came from the passenger cabin of the plane. Allan couldn't tell if it came from the machines or the animals, but it didn't matter. Whatever it was, it reminded Allan to stay calm. He sat in the co-pilot's chair and looked at the black sky. The lights of the city-New Haven, he supposed-were very strong and almost illuminated the clouds that passed overhead. The lights of houses and cars went past the windshield like a parade of glow worms. That would have been really annoying if he was working, but right now it released an incredible serenity in Allan.

As his head leaned against the back of the seat, he was already asleep.

A Hero

A loud knock startled Allan, and he jumped up. Something had slammed against the door, causing it to buckle even more. Then he remembered where he was, what he had to do. He looked at the control panel and tried to determine the plane's location.

The first rays of sunlight weren't enough for him to understand. He rubbed his eyes and managed to make out an undulating glitter. The 747 was crossing over Lake Ontario. The time had come.

"Let's play," Allan said, admiring his own courage. He took a deep breath and began initiating the landing plan. Two sparks came out of the control panel. The plane didn't seem to be following his commands.

Allan paused. This couldn't be happening. He immediately checked to see if he could dump the fuel, but the switch was destroyed. He tried futilely to repair it. The problem gradually became more complicated. The only thing he could do was to try to find another way to empty the plane's fuel tanks. Otherwise, he would have to keep the plane circling until the inevitable occurred.

He was about to try the second idea when a sudden shake made him hang onto his seat. "We've already run out of fuel," he thought, but didn't know whether or not he should be glad.

The plane's altitude was already decreasing. In a minute they'd hit the surface of the water.

Allan looked for the last time at the world he was going to leave. He heard a second knock behind him, but he ignored it. He wanted his last minutes to be serene, slow. A tear trickled down his cheek and he raised his hand to wipe it off. He wasn't sorry for himself; he was just worried about his sister, his only relative in the world.

In front of him, the blue waves on the water were coming closer and closer. Only ten seconds before the end. Allan closed his eyes and waited. Then, he felt hot breath against his face.

The creatures were standing in front of him. He wasn't afraid. He simply smiled at them and said, "You're coming with me!"

They jumped into the air, charging at him. They collided, sending Allan as well as the creatures against the windshield. It shattered.

Allan saw them growl, howl and then...vast darkness descended in front of his eyes. He died shouting inside, "I'm somebody!"

TO LAUGH OR TO CRY?

The light marking the 747 on the gigantic screen in the White House went off. Clive approached the screen slowly, without taking his eyes from the spot. When he got right in front of the screen, he was certain. The 747's flight ended just before the Canadian shore of Lake Ontario, and that could mean only one thing.

He felt happiness and sorrow all at the same time. Because of the four hundred and fifty wasted lives on the 747, four hundred and fifty other lives had been saved.

For unknown reasons, the Boeing hadn't followed its predefined course. Those were the exact words that would be printed in the newspapers the next day, the words that would be heard that night on the news.

"Make this unfortunate event public," the Defense Secretary said in a strange, mild tone. "It could be much worse, Clive," he added, "much worse!"

And yes, indeed, those two knew very well that it could be much worse!

THE LAST DAYS BEFORE THE CRISIS...

And if you looked at the name human…
you…you could never hear whispers

NEW YORK CITY

"…Daniel, it's now your turn to tell us when the Cretaceous period was!" The teacher wore a sarcastic, almost aggressive expression. He knew very well who had studied in every lesson.

The twelve-year-old boy thought he should at least try to answer.

"Two hundred thousand years B.C. to…" The teacher's look changed. The boy realized he was wrong.

"Note that next time, you'll write two hundred times for me that the Cretaceous period fell between 135 million years and sixty-five million years ago."

Daniel lifted his pen and started writing. He was very angry. He scribbled his notes immediately after the teacher turned his back.

He'd never liked dinosaurs. The chapters related to them were added to the class textbook right after he joined the class, and he considered it one of the greatest misfortunes of his life. He used to call dinosaurs thick-skinned, dirty lizards. But worst of all was the unlimited hatred the teacher displayed toward Daniel himself. Not once had he ever said a good word for Daniel. Maybe Daniel's indifference toward those creatures that lived sixty-five million years ago was to blame for that. His disdain for those creatures that thrilled every child of that time!

"What did I say right now, Daniel?" the teacher asked, interrupting Daniel's thoughts.

The classmate sitting behind Daniel whispered the answer to him.

"You were talking about the split of Laurasia, sir," the boy answered, but the teacher ignored him. He kept talking without giving any notice to Daniel. "Maybe if I had given the wrong answer, the reaction would be more direct," Daniel thought as he watched the teacher write the words *Gondwana* and *Laurasia* on the blackboard.

"At the time these two landmasses were broken into more continents, quite a few species of dinosaurs existed. Amongst them, tyrannosaurus and deinonychus, triceratops and apatosaurus. Those four animals dominated not only during the Cretaceous period but also in people's minds, because they are characteristic of the groups they belong to." He stopped talking for a moment and turned his back to the students to write his notes on the blackboard. The kids started talking to each other in low voices.

"Write down in your workbooks what's on the blackboard," the teacher added, but no one seemed to have heard him. Only one girl paid attention to his words, immediately opening her notebook.

Nancy was always careful in her classes. She would lock herself in her room and wouldn't come out until she had finished all her homework. Her teachers recognized her efforts. So did Daniel. He was almost the only one who didn't tease her for her attitude. He and Nancy were very good friends, only they didn't even know it yet!

"What are you writing down there, Miss Jerk?" a boy from the back desk shouted.

Nancy didn't give him any notice. The teacher sharply turned his head in an attempt to spot the culprit. He gave the impression he knew who it was, without, however, upbraiding the guilty student, who sank down in his seat and looked indifferent.

"Now I want you to open your textbooks and to page fifty-two." The class followed his instructions. "Nancy, read from the middle of the page downwards."

55

"From the point where it says triceratops, sir?," the girl asked. The teacher nodded and sat down, placing his own book on the desk.

"Triceratops, herbivore," Nancy read clearly. "It lived during the Cretaceous period, approximately 144 to 65 million years ago. It reached lengths of twenty-seven feet and weighed approximately five tons. Its characteristic element was a large osteal chlamys on the back of its head."

"It is possible that this cranial cover was utilized as a shield against bloodthirsty carnivorous predators, protecting the neck and the body. It could also work as an intimidation element against enemies, a practice that is also exhibited by some lizard species.

"Triceratops roamed in herds, migrating from one place to another. This opinion is based on the fact that many fossils of triceratops were found gathered in one place. Imagine these animals alive, running together, destroying everything in their path. A real Cretaceous scene," she finished reading.

"Very well," the teacher told Nancy, "go on," but the student had already started.

"Brachiosaurus, herbivore. Weighing over sixty tons with a length of sixty-six feet, it is considered to have been one of the largest dinosaurs that ever lived. This bulky creature must have used its tail as a means of defense. A blow from it upon any carnivore would send it several feet away and smash some of its bones. The long neck must have been intended either to reach the leaves of tall trees or to keep its head out of the water when the animal waded.

"Although brachiosaurus was a strong animal, it doesn't seem to have had any aggressive attitudes. Its life was mostly calm and serene, although the sound of its walk startled all the other creatures of the Cretaceous period." Nancy took a deep breath and continued.

"Deinonychus. Bloodthirsty carnivore that didn't depend on its height of seven and a half to ten and a half feet, but on its great swiftness and intelligence. Its appellation arose, of course, from its appallingly sharp sickle claw.

"These animals hunted in groups, while they always kept an ace up their sleeve. They would pounce on their live prey and snap at the flesh, hooking it with their claws and tearing it apart with their sharp teeth. Their victim would fall and, unable to react, would only wait for its slow death!

"Deinonychus is the first member of a homologue chain named Deinonychosaurs. Other predators like dromaeosaurus and velociraptor also belong to this species. All of them were simply invincible."

At that moment the bell rang, forcing Nancy to stop reading. The children grabbed their school bags and ran out of the class. The girl, left behind, slowly prepared her own bag.

She fastened the zipper and hung it on her shoulder. But then she was surprised to realize that Daniel was standing in front of her.

"I thought that maybe we could go downstairs together," he said.

"You know, I stopped reading just before the most interesting subject of the book!"

"What subject?" the boy asked.

"Well, I took a look before putting my book back in my bag."

"And what's this subject about?" Daniel asked.

Nancy gave him a mischievous look. "The greatest hunter of all time. The only real killer nature has created!" she answered as they separated, each going his own way.

CLARA-PROGRAM

The image on her computer screen changed. Clara reached out and lifted the cup by her right hand. She moved the mouse, selecting the program she wanted, and a "loading" message appeared on the screen.

At that moment, the doorbell rung.

Clara rose and headed towards the door as if she had been expecting the sound.

"Welcome home, sweetie," she said as she opened the door. Nancy walked in quickly and threw her bag on the couch. "How did it go today?"" She sat down in front of the computer again.

"Fine," the girl answered, but she didn't seem to mean it. Her mother ignored it. After all, Nancy's attitude was the same every day.

Her mother supposed it was due to the way her classmates treated her. As she had herself confessed, she was one of the best students in class, so it was natural that the other kids, not exactly examples of kindness, would tease her and laugh at her. Nancy had reached the point of wondering whether it was worth it to be a good student.

"I can see you got the computer back, mum," she said as she drew near. "Does it work?"

Her mother nodded. "They finally managed to remove the virus. You can't imagine how much it cost me," Clara added.

"What are you doing there?" Nancy asked as her mother pressed some keys.

"I'm checking to see if there's anything lost from the hard disk."

Nancy's face assumed an odd look. "Mum, did you buy what I asked for?" she asked and immediately saw Clara's expression grow curious.

"What are you talking about, Nancy?"

"How could you forget?" the girl whined.

"Calm down, I'm only kidding you," Clara said, and pulled a small parallelogram box from her handbag.

Nancy grabbed it right away. "You're the best!" she shouted and kissed her mother. "Can I load it now?" she asked impatiently.

"Of course," Clara said and took the computer back to the desktop screen.

Nancy opened the box, laid the thick manual on the table, and inserted the disk in the DVD-ROM. The installation process started; it would be complete in less than a minute.

Nancy waited anxiously while the computer restarted. Finally the setup was confirmed and the program ready to run. Without hesitating, Nancy selected the new icon and a new window replaced the desktop.

"What interests you most in this title?" her mother asked her.

"Whatever has to do with dinosaurs thrills me; you know that."

"It can't be just that; something must have caught your attention for you to want it so much."

"You're never wrong," Nancy said, smiling. Her computer screen displayed a catalogue of choices, but the girl wasn't searching at random. The mouse cursor passed over all the other words and immediately stopped at *Biotechnology: the Theory of Regeneration!*

Endless columns of letters and information appeared on the screen. Nancy, either out of bad habit or curiosity, moved the cursor to the end of the text to read the last sentence-the outcome of all the previous pages. She read it out loud, unaware that the words were coming out of her lips.

"Therefore, despite some insufficient, scattered and scarce ambiguities, the theory's implementation has been described as impossible, while its future doesn't appear to be too bright!"

A FEW DAYS LATER

"Hi Daniel, it's me," a voice said on the phone.

"Nancy, you called for the schoolwork, right?"

"Of course I called for the schoolwork. We arranged to go together."

"I remember, I remember. I can drop by your house in an hour."

"The library is closer to your house, Daniel!"

"You mean, you'll come by my house?" the boy wondered.

"Don't forget to take a pen and a workbook," Nancy said.

"Okay, but…"

"I'll be there in ten minutes," the girl said, and hung up.

"Nancy, are you listening?" Daniel asked, but of course he got no answer. He put the phone down, irritated. He didn't like being ignored at all, especially when he couldn't react.

Less than five minutes later, Daniel heard the doorbell ring. "She's too fast," he thought, "she must be in a hurry to meet me." He grabbed a workbook and a pencil and went downstairs and out the door. Nancy was waiting for him fifteen feet away.

"You're too slow," she said and started walking quickly down the sidewalk. Daniel didn't speak at all.

She set an unusually fast pace. Trying to keep up with her he didn't pay much attention to the questions she asked every once in a while. He left her to soliloquize.

"…Daniel, I think you're not listening to me."

"Yes," the boy answered.

"Now I'm sure!"

"Sure?" Daniel pretended to wonder.

"You're really ignoring me," she said. When he absently said "yes" again, she stopped talking.

They finally reached the library entrance. They walked in noiselessly. Nancy whispered to Daniel, "Give me your I.D. and follow me."

They walked slowly and quietly through the thousands of stacked books. A bookshelf filled with large binders immediately caught Daniel's attention. Each was marked with a range of dates. He opened one and realized the binders contained clippings of headline stories from various newspapers. He was fascinated.

He thought it wouldn't matter if he spent some time leafing through one of them. He stretched out his hand and randomly took down the one labeled *December-November 1997.*

Nancy walked up and down in front of a shelf of books, trying to choose one to read. She stopped and chose a book. It was covered in dust, like the ones Daniel had in his room. She held it out in both her hands and blew the dust off, creating a cloud that made her sneeze twice.

She placed the book on a big table and sat on a chair before it to start browsing through the pages, but a voice interrupted her.

"Nancy, where are you?" Daniel shouted.

She suddenly realized she had forgotten him, and right after that, she wished she didn't know him.

"Nancy," Daniel shouted again when she didn't answer.

Someone would eventually turn up and throw him out, Nancy thought; after all, they were in a library. She certainly didn't want to follow him. All she wanted was to finish her schoolwork.

"I found you at last," Daniel said when he rounded a bookshelf and saw Nancy in front of him.

"You're completely stupid, Daniel," Nancy told him. Daniel's face took on a look of bafflement. "You're shouting as if we're out in the street!"

"Save that and come with me!"

"Lower your voice, or they'll throw us out!"

"All right, I will," Daniel said in a lower voice, "if you follow me." He took her hand and Nancy, unable to do otherwise, let him guide her to another area in the vast room.

"What is it that you find so remarkable here?" Nancy asked. Daniel gave her a contemptuous look. Then he showed her the binder he had opened on a table. The girl got closer.

"Three dead women and a dead man..." she read one of the lines in the article out loud. "So what?" she said as if that was normal, "so many people die every day."

"Yes," the boy said, "but this was the first time someone died like that." He pointed at a photograph with his finger.

The girl frowned. The photo told much more than what had been printed in the article. The body that was lying in the middle of the road was half-eaten, tattered. There was no doubt that a very strange animal had attacked the unfortunate woman. But it was bizarre. How could such a vicious animal have appeared in the center of Buenos Aires? It was almost impossible.

"Whatever attacked her dismembered her, and the limbs weren't found anywhere. They're most likely still in the stomach of the blood-thirsty creature that attacked her," Daniel observed.

Nancy, on hearing these words, moved away. She tried to find a logical explanation. "Did you go through the other newspapers? The creature might have been caught and-" Daniel shook his head and she broke off. Both looked at the photo again.

"Unprecedented savageness," she whispered, unaware of the importance of the words she spoke.

Whatever had killed that woman, the third victim that night, had acted swiftly and intelligently. Those two words made her freeze. She was sure she had heard them somewhere before.

At that moment, she noticed two holes in the victims back. They were deep and located right under the neck. She shuddered.

The only word heard from her lips was…"Deinonychus!"

THE PAST MAKES THE FUTURE

The doorbell rang six times in quick succession. Whoever waited beyond the door was definitely impatient. Clara, Nancy's mother, opened the door without looking to see who it was. Her eyes remained on the television just a few feet away. She saw Nancy walk over the threshold out of the tail of her eye.

"Mum, you can't imagine what Daniel and I found in the library today!" Nancy exclaimed, but her mother wasn't listening; she signaled Nancy to be silent. She moved closer to the TV and turned the volume up.

"The investigation of the cause of this terrible accident is still underway. However, according to first estimates, the plane must now be at a depth of about six hundred feet. We should have the answers to the questions that have arisen shortly."

Nancy, still next to the TV, turned the volume down again. "Mum, when I tell you what Daniel and I discovered today, you're not going to believe it!" Clara's look revealed to Nancy that her mother was ignoring her words. "I think you're not listening. I'll tell you anyway and you can believe whatever you want."

"What do you want?" Clara asked.

"I'm not sure yet, but I think-"

"If you're not sure yet, come and tell me what you want when you are sure," Clara said and walked into the kitchen. Nancy didn't speak, but stayed still and wondered what all of this could mean.

And it was only then that she realized that all the deaths, all the accidents, were only the beginning. The beginning of the end!

BARRY
SIDNEY

A thump was heard every once in a while. Barry killed time by throwing a tennis ball against the white wall in front of him. Actually, all the walls here were white. One's eyes could forget the colors of the outside world. The hours in a mental hospital didn't just seem endless, they were endless.

He sighed and lay on his bed once more. He looked at the ceiling, trying to find something different, something worthy of the meaningless time at his disposal. He wondered if he was really insane or not. There was one thing he knew for sure, however; he had seen the creature with his own eyes, not his imagination, just as he had seen his friend die, helpless, unable to fight for his life.

Someone who wanted to wear him down and make him question his own mind had locked him up where he was now.

On the right side of his bed was a pile of books, all about dinosaurs. He had read them again and again, and had ended up an expert on that subject. Besides the books, as he used to say, he had personal experience with dinosaurs!

On the wall a bit farther away, several beautifully-framed paintings broke the monotony of the room. They all displayed similar images: a gray-hued animal with a long tail and yellow eyes posing amongst thousands of corpses.

Many things ran through Barry's mind. He had plenty of time to rank the thoughts into important and trivial categories. But in all that, there was one fact that stood out. It was the last scene of a life that didn't resemble the one he was leading now. It was the eyes, the movements, the desperate voice of his friend as he died under the attack of the vicious predator. Barry had survived because his friend Jimmy had died. That's what he believed and that belief was the impetus that plunged him even deeper into this cell than anything else had.

Barry simply didn't believe that he deserved to live. He hadn't tried at all to avoid being committed to the mental institution; he nearly helped them get him into it. That was, of course, the most convenient way for NeoGene to close his record.

Barry was dead on paper. The people in the institute called him Barry simply because he had told them that that was the name he would answer to. However, he was recorded in the files as "unknown" while outside, in society, he was listed as dead. He had been erased from the world, and worse, he wasn't willing to get back into it.

The ball bounced against the wall once more, making a loud sound quite out of place in the quiet institution. No matter how much he rejected other people, Barry longed for the fuss of the streets, the rows of buildings and the crowds. It had been so long since he had experienced these simple things that he wished he had been more observant of them when he'd had the opportunity. "The worst thing is that you can never know when it's going to be your last time," he thought to himself.

He left the ball lying on his leg. He picked up a book and started browsing through it, turning the pages so fast that he seemed to be just looking at the pictures without paying any attention to the text. He suddenly stopped. The page he was looking at showed a carnivorous dinosaur-a predator-leaning over its prey.

He stared at the picture. More than a minute later, he suddenly closed the book and threw it forcefully against the wall in front of him.

"We're all going to die," he said in a low voice, then added, "And that day won't be too far away."

CLIVE

WASHINGTON

At the same moment…

It had been forty-eight hours since he had last slept. His face was all red, while his head felt unusually heavy. Despite all that, Clive was still standing. He had been forced by these difficult circumstances to remain so.

He leaned forward in his seat and held his head in his hands. In all the fuss, he heard some thumps in front of him. He lifted his head and saw Foster place his hands on the table and look at him, troubled.

"Is there any problem?" Clive asked in a faint voice. He sounded half dead.

Foster shook his head, which didn't appease Clive at all.

"Is there something you want to tell me?" Clive asked.

Foster glanced right, then left before he spoke. "You know, I lied to you before. There is indeed a problem."

Clive didn't speak but only closed his eyes, waiting to hear what else could go wrong that day.

"You're that problem Clive," Foster said in an aggressive tone, "you and your actions. From the first moment you became President of the United States, you've been making one mistake after the other."

Clive shoved his chair back and abruptly stood up. "How dare you?"

"Exactly like you dared!" Foster retorted.

"Do you know who you're talking to right now? Do you know I gave you this position and I'm ready to take it back?"

"Don't be so sure Clive. You don't have so much power as you imagine. You're not the only one in this government!"

"What do you mean by that?" Clive said suspiciously. "You can't do something like what you're thinking-you'll go down with me!"

"I'm not thinking anything yet."

"If this gets out..."

"What are you going to do?" Foster challenged, "kill me?"

"You're just trying to avoid any blame for this terrible accident!"

"It might have been an accident for some, but not for you. You know this didn't accidentally happen!"

"I can't be sure!"

"No, Clive. You are simply reserving this incident as an excuse in case something goes wrong!"

"You knew all that. You'll also be considered responsible, and your career will be ruined!"

"I know that much better than you do, so you don't have to be afraid. I'm not going to reveal anything."

"Keep it down," Clive said as he heard his name called.

"Mr. Clive." An aide interrupted their conversation. "We have problems."

"You can go now, Foster. I don't need you any more," the president said and immediately turned to listen to the aide.

"The team selected to determine the cause of the accident..."

"What happened to them?"

"Well, look; they've stopped above the spot where the Boeing sank, but they can't go on," the aide said hesitantly. "You see, the weather bureau is forecasting worsening weather conditions that will prohibit investigation of the crash."

"That's bad, too bad," the president said, and turned to look at Foster. He smiled.

THE STORM

The first bolt of lightning brightened the New York sky. The rain tapped on the window of Daniel's room, keeping him awake. He thought it was that monotonous sound that disturbed him, but he wasn't sure.

He rose from his bed and turned on the light, then tried to look outside the window. The room's light created images on the glass so annoying that he eventually turned the light off again. Everything outside was dark.

The rain was now falling heavily, pounding so that you felt it more than heard it. In spots, the darkness hid some of the millions of raindrops, while in other spots, it didn't. Daniel saw a car driving down the street. It went slowly and carefully. Its strong headlights made the rain appear and disappear. Daniel knew the rain was there; the fact he was unable to see it didn't mean it didn't exist, but then, that applied to many other things, too-more dangerous things.

The beams from the car's headlights stroked some trees in Central Park. In their brief light, the boy saw raindrops falling on the soil, into the grass and...he froze. He had also seen something else in that short period of time. But what could that something be that had caused him to hold his breath?

In the lights of the car, Daniel had seen a mark, a footprint, imprinted on the wet soil. It wasn't a human footprint; it looked more like the foot of an unusually large bird. "What could its presence in such a big city mean?" he wondered and suddenly remembered the newspaper clippings he had read at the library. He shuddered.

He listened carefully for any strange sound, but the rain drowned everything out. He thought that maybe he hadn't seen clearly. Besides, he was influenced by the conversation he had had with Nancy earlier that day. Maybe his imagination was creating all of this.

However, he couldn't convince himself that everything was all right. He didn't at all like the idea that there was a dinosaur in the park where he grew up.

He grew courageous enough to move away from his place at the window. He crept silently to the door and locked it, turning the key twice. He was on the edge of panic; he didn't know what he should do, what his next action would be. He wanted to scream, run away, hide, do whatever it would take to turn that creature away from him. He was certain now that he wasn't mistaken in what he'd seen.

He slowly sat down on his bed and, terrified, put his hands over his face. His fear had turned into such a real nightmare that he had visions. Overwhelmed, he couldn't think what move he should make next. He stayed very still and quiet.

He dropped his hands and looked left and right but didn't see anything. He knew he could be wrong, but what if what he had seen belonged to a dinosaur? The worst of thoughts went through his mind.

Quite some time had passed since he'd seen the footprint and Daniel's breathing grew more and more normal. He was still afraid but managed to quell his panic for the time being. His heart still beat loudly, but not as fast as earlier, and merely assured him that he was still alive.

He wanted to find out what time it was but he knew he shouldn't move. Deep inside, he believed and hoped that it had been hours since he had frozen in his position on the bed. He didn't intend to move from there until dawn! Four more hours was no big deal, he told himself, especially since he already must have stayed still for that long. So he sat still where he was, waiting impatiently for some sign of dawn, some sunbeam that would tell him that his torment was coming to an end.

But it was only midnight!

WITH THE FIRST SUNRAY

His legs hung over the edge of the bed. Lying sloppily on his quilt, he looked tired and sweaty. The first sunbeams entered his window, lightening the room just enough that he woke up. Daniel put his hand in front of his eyes, irritated by the light. Then he remembered what had happened.

He suddenly sat up in his bed, realizing he had fallen asleep. That didn't bother him too much now, since he was still alive. His legs were numb. He started moving them, then stopped when he remembered that he shouldn't make any noise. He stood up and slowly and carefully moved towards the door.

Soundlessly, he turned the handle and attempted to push the door open, then remembered it was locked; he'd locked it himself the night before. He finally stepped out of his room and looked around. It didn't seem like anyone else was awake. He slowly went down the stairs, constantly looking back and forth. The first thing he wanted to do was check whether that footprint he had seen last night was real.

He opened the front door and stepped into the garden. The sunlight momentarily blinded him, but then he saw what a beautiful day it was.

Daniel heard a bird's twitter, but he didn't care about anything except what had troubled him for the past eleven hours, what had taught him fear, since he was only twelve years old!

He crossed the wide avenue that separated his house and Central Park. He tread quickly over to the bare patch of dirt that held the sole clue to whatever had been there the previous night. He leaned down, blocking the light with his body so the ground was shaded. He was surprised. There was nothing there. No trace; no footprint.

Joy filled him and made his face glow. There was no danger, no reason for anymore nightmares. A second later, he realized that the rain had washed away the footprint. But it hadn't reached another spot, under the trees, where there were not one but three footprints!

ANNIHILATION

"Nancy," Daniel said into the phone in a voice more scared than excited. "Listen to me. You must come here right away. It's urgent. Bye." He hung the phone up.

Daniel was shocked by everything going on around him. He'd locked himself in his room and he couldn't stop crying. He was convinced that his time had come. Nancy was his last hope, the only person who could believe him and understand him.

Nancy rang the doorbell and waited for someone to open the door. "She must be Daniel's mother," the girl thought when a beautiful woman opened the door.

"Hello. I'm Daniel's classmate…"

" Try to calm him down my dear, I beg you. He's been jabbering since this morning."

"I'll do my best," Nancy answered as she entered.

"His room is at the end of the hall, on your right," the woman said, pointing the way.

Nancy walked to the door and knocked. "Daniel, it's me, Nancy. Open the door."

She heard the door unlock and then Daniel signaled for her to get in fast. She stepped hesitantly into the room. Daniel locked the door again.

"Why all these precautions?" she asked.

Daniel looked at her with red eyes. "The predator," he stammered.

"What do you mean?"

"I saw it, Nancy! It was here last night," Daniel said.

No one spoke for quite some time.

"Are you sure?" Nancy asked.

"Stop that. Why should I lie? Why does everyone think I'm lying?"

"Calm down, that's not what I meant. Just tell me exactly what happened last night."

"Come with me," the boy said. "You'd better see for yourself in order to believe it."

Nancy looked at him curiously. "Why haven't you shown it to anyone else? Please, I can't be the only one to know."

Eventually Nancy agreed to follow him.

They both stood as if frozen, staring at the barely discernible footprints.

"It's amazing," Nancy said.

"No, it's horrible," Daniel corrected her.

"You didn't make these, did you?" she asked. Daniel shook his head. "Did you by any chance see what made them?"

"Nancy, if I had seen the animal that left these tracks, I wouldn't have stopped running. Anyway, no matter what left them, I don't like it at all!"

"I can't-I can't believe it. The toes, these claws…I don't know, but they seem to me like those of…"

"That's exactly what I thought," Daniel interrupted. "We can't be both imagining this."

"Daniel, this could be a prank, or something formed completely accidentally."

"Three times?"

"What did you say?"

"There are three footprints on the ground."

"You're right…but even in that case my first proposal still stands."

"I don't know."

"You can't know," Nancy retorted.

"Maybe you're right. But what if you're wrong?" he said, and of course there was no answer, there couldn't be one. "Nancy this might sound stupid but…"

"What do you want?"

"Well, listen, could I sleep at your place tonight?" Daniel asked.

"Of course, but why?"

"I don't know," Daniel muttered.

"What do you mean, you don't know?"

"I mean I don't know. It was you who said one can't always know."

"Yes."

"So, the same feeling that makes me think these footprints are real makes me not want to sleep here tonight."

"What can I say, if it's so important to you?"

"Thank you."

"Big deal. Just don't be under the illusion that you'll be safer at my place, if something indeed exists out here."

"At least I'll be close to you," Daniel replied.

"What did you say?"

"I'm saying I'll definitely be safer."

"Why is that?" she asked and looked at him quizzically.

The boy thought about it for a while and then answered, "Well, if you noticed, these footprints point right across to my house."

"Ooh! That's what you said, right?"

"Why, isn't that enough?"

"It's more than enough," she said, staring at him. "Well, you know something, Daniel?"

"What?"

"We two must be joined with something more than a mere secret," she said and smiled.

It was a unique smile: bright, precious, and the last one.

Just Before The Outbreak!

Daniel pressed a button on the remote control and the television changed channels.

"Nothing interesting," Nancy heard him say. He reached out and picked up a magazine. He turned the pages, giving Nancy the impression that he was looking for something.

"What did your parents say about our discovery?" he asked.

"I didn't tell them," Nancy looked at Daniel. "How about yours?"

"I've told you. Nobody believed me; I saw that in my mother's eyes. It's dreadful to see someone trying to reason with you when they're the one who's wrong. We reached the point where my mother called my father on the ship to calm me down-to calm down the one who knows the truth!"

"And what's the truth, Daniel?"

"I wish I knew," he said and looked at the ceiling as though staring right through it to the sky beyond.

Nancy leaned close to him. "Daniel, how come everyone who wonders about the truth of the world lifts his head up and searches the stars?"

"Maybe that's where the truth is hidden-out there somewhere." He looked at Nancy and saw a tear trickle down her cheek. "What's wrong?" he asked.

"I'm very worried, Daniel."

"What for?" He took her hand and held it tightly in his own. "There, look in front of you. You see there's no sky to look into, just a concrete wall; a wall we've built."

" Bloodthirsty predators; hostile, unfeeling figures; creatures that live but can't appreciate life," Nancy said, with closed eyes.

"You've memorized the book," Daniel said, and laughed.

"No," she replied, startled, "anything but that; those words came from you. They're your reaction, your fear. When I found you in your room, you looked exhausted and terrified."

At that moment, the big wooden door opened. Nancy hastily left Daniel's embrace when her mother walked into the house.

Clara probably didn't even see her. She carried a heavy bag in one hand and her handbag hung from on her other shoulder. "Mum, I've told you not to come home so late; it's dangerous," Nancy admonished her.

"I can see you weren't left alone."

"I told you over the phone that Daniel is sleeping over with us tonight," Nancy reminded her.

Daniel stood up and greeted Nancy's mother.

"I remember," she said, then addressed Daniel. "Have you informed your parents, my boy?" When Daniel nodded, Clara left the bag and her handbag on an armchair and went to her bedroom.

The boy looked at Nancy. "Your mother seems nice. Definitely better than mine, anyway."

"Why do you say that?"

Daniel laughed bitterly. "It's a long story," he said and looked away, toward the wall.

"You don't care for her at all."

"Of course I care, she's my mother!" Daniel said. "Only a monster wouldn't care about its mother."

"A predator," Nancy said thoughtfully.

"Yes, a predator, like…"

"Like deinonychus, or velociraptor…"

"Whatever else we think, we always end up in the same conversation. We're become obsessed," Daniel said. "We've most probably made all this up with our imaginations."

"You're right. Besides, we can't be the only ones on the whole planet who know the truth."

"Now it all seems funny to me," Daniel said, and laughed. "We were just being stupid, after all."

"I don't like to hear that, but you're probably right," Nancy admitted.

"At least you didn't tell anyone, but I did."

"Yeah, yeah …" Nancy said absently. Her words didn't correspond with the expression on her face. She looked doubtful.

" Nancy, what's wrong?"

"What do you mean?"

"You don't believe what you're saying. I can see it."

"You've got that right, Daniel."

"Why?" the boy asked. His tone had changed, too. He didn't sound confident anymore.

"I wish…I wish I knew and could tell you!" Nancy exclaimed.

They fell silent for a few moments.

"Do you know something?" Nancy suddenly said. "We all do the same thing."

"What's that?"

"We close our eyes…and wait. That's all we do."

"It's not very nice, to hear that."

"No, it's not nice at all, but…"

"But what?" Daniel prompted.

"Well, I had a funny idea."

"Since it's your idea, I want to hear it."

"Maybe we could correct something," Nancy said.

Daniel laughed. "I don't know why, but something deep inside me is telling me it's too late!"

"Daniel, you're scaring me." Nancy's voice quavered.

"Maybe that's the solution."

Now Nancy was confused. "What are you talking about?"

"Fear, Nancy," he said, looking into her eyes. "Maybe fear is the final solution!"

THE CRISIS

Merely at the scream...
There!
The tears of your world told me!
There you'll be taken aback!

KNOWING THE FUTURE

Nancy lifted the remote control from the table in front of her. She looked at Daniel. "Maybe" "we should tell more people after all," she said. "Someone will believe us; someone will show interest."

Then she turned the television on.

They stared at the TV screen with their mouths open. They didn't make a sound, just watched the TV program, frozen in place.

"And you can see here," a news reporter was saying, "all that's left of the poor woman. Her adopted son, Daniel Wimpley, is missing."

Those words were enough to make the boy realize that it was his house on the television screen, and his stepmother who had been found dead, almost half eaten. A tear trickled down his cheek.

He considered what would have happened to him if he had stayed at his house that night. A second teardrop dripped onto his shirt. But this time the tear was caused by something different. This time, he cried because he was still alive.

"I was right," he murmured.

"Yes Daniel, you were right," Nancy said.

He touched his face with his hands and then hid his eyes. At some point, he'd stood up; now his legs wouldn't hold him any longer and he dropped to the floor. "She's dead," he said, almost to himself. "My mother's gone once more...why me?"

"Daniel…" Nancy sat down beside him on the floor. She reached for him and begged him to stop crying. "Oh my god, his mother dead, in front of my eyes," she said, and her vision blurred.

And darkness pours as the stars go out
Souls of people, many, worthless
And hope vanishes in the light of a night
Long, endless, beginning of a day

Daniel was bemused. Thousands of thoughts overwhelmed his mind; none of them comforting, none would soften his pain. Among them was a sound, words from the world outside his mind. He slowly raised his head and looked at the television. The screen's glare hurt his eyes. On it, a newscaster talked into the camera.

"This is the fifth murder that has come to light in a very short period of-"

He changed the channel.

"…no one knows how many more people will die…"

"…Sidney was traumatized by three similar murd…"

"…Sidney and Buenos Aires seem to feel for…"

"…sixth victim outside Central…"

"…what animal does these…"

"…we all pray for the people that have died, and for those who may die. We still don't know what is killing these people, but we're sure we'll find out, and then only God knows what the result of the people's rage will be!"

Daniel turned the television off. He saw Nancy's mother standing in the doorway staring at him. He and Nancy looked at each other.

"There'll be panic," the girl said, and a terrifying silence filled the house.

PANIC

"What the hell is happening here?" Clive shouted. He'd just been informed that a fifteenth victim, the fifteenth in two hours, had been reported in New York. "What kind of creature on this earth could do such execrable things?"

"I'm afraid it's not just one, Clive," his friend Vincent Winslow said. "New York isn't the only city where people are being attacked. There are two more places that we know of: Buenos Aires and Sydney. The television news reporters discovered the similarities and linked the deaths before we did. But, there's something more that bothers me."

"Say it; what worse could there be?"

"Listen," Winslow said, "I think you'll agree with me. In all cases, parts of the victims are missing-eaten. A small animal wouldn't eat that much. If there is only one animal, then there would be two, maybe as many as thirteen victims attributable to it. However, it would have to be very large, or very plentiful. Either one large animal or a large number of animals would have been detected."

"What are you getting at?"

"What I want to say, Mr. President, is two things. First, that it's not merely a carnivorous animal but a serial killer. Secondly, there's a chance that it has a den inside Central Park, where it feeds its young!"

Clive stared at him.

"Mr. President," an aide called from the other side of the room. Clive turned in that direction.

"They've announced the sixteenth in a row; the woman was found a while ago in a pool of blood."

The president's eyes half-closed. "This is it," Clive said. "Call for military units; I want at least two satellites to focus on the area; tell the governments of Argentina and Australia to do the same. We'll get the damned things, whatever it takes. We'll get them and make them spit all the blood that they've sucked from every American citizen."

"Sir, it's most likely that the other governments will ask permission to restore operation of their military satellites," the aide said. "Australia doesn't possess any others that can detect and record the attacks."

"Put them straight through to my office. I'll negotiate with them from there."

"Yes, sir" the aide said, and left hastily.

"Is there anything else that needs my attention?"

"Not for the time being."

"I'll be in my office; report to me every five minutes."

"Yes, Mr. President" the officer in charge said, and Clive withdrew to his office.

Central Park Mission

A bright circle of light swept over the small forest. The sound of a helicopter reverberated in the streets of Manhattan. The darkness made the mission even more difficult. The searchlights that intermittently penetrated the leaves of the trees weren't enough to help.

The area had been evacuated for quite some time. Several police and army vehicles had been placed around the forested area to block the escape of the bloodthirsty animals, whatever those were.

However, nothing can ever be perfect.A military unit walked quickly between the blockades that had been set up, drawing ever closer to the park. Their combined tread was so heavy that one would think they carried all the weaponry available. The atmosphere was anything but calm. Scattered words were heard from every direction, fragments of conversations expressing worry and concern. The area outside the park was sufficiently illuminated but that stopped among the first trees. The unit's objective was to find the creature that had caused all those deaths, and exterminate it.

The ten soldiers walked through the last roadblock of cars and tanks. Little by little, they melted into the darkness of what was formerly the most frequented park in the world. None of them glanced back to the lights, the people, the life they left behind. Maybe because they simply didn't know that it would be their last opportunity to see any of those things.

The unit's officer moved his hands, signaling to the unit to separate into two groups. They did so, and the two groups moved off in different directions. If they'd known the power of their opponent, they would have stuck together.

Beneath the foliage of the tall trees, he soldiers walked slowly. Electricity in the greater part of the park had been knocked out the night before, during the sudden storm. It was supposed to have been repaired that afternoon but events had delayed the repairs. The soldiers were forced to use infrared goggles and walk step-by-step, a situation not applicable to the predators.

No, they could see much better, no matter whether it was night or day, and they had already tracked the soldiers down!

A branch snapped loudly. The soldier who had stepped on it slowly lifted his boot to avoid making any more noise, and followed the man in front of him, gun at the ready. A breeze blew, cooling the soldiers' sweaty faces.

One of them closed his eyes, enjoying the cool sensation. Suddenly he felt something slide quickly, almost inconspicuously across his chest, and then...then he realized that his chest had been ripped open. His last breath fell from his lips like water falling from a waterfall, never to come back, and thus he passed away.

The heavy equipment hanging from his back prevented another soldier from walking easily. He was following the man in front of him mechanically, without thinking what he was doing. At one point, he glanced back and...froze.

Nobody was following him. The others had all disappeared.

He quickly looked forward, panicky, and saw the other soldier walking about twelve feet ahead and gradually vanishing into the darkness. He wanted to shout, but realized he shouldn't. He thought that maybe they should have followed a different method to inspect the park, maybe they ought to have evacuated it the usual way, but then he realized it was too late to worry about any of that. If the creatures really existed, then it was likely that they were close to him. The less noticeable his presence was, the better for him.

The lead soldier kept walking further into the darkness without realizing that no one followed him. The other group had not moved. The only thing they would hear was the sough of the leaves in the light breeze and an imperceptible murmur coming from the people outside the park.

He didn't know what to do. He seemed to have lost the courage he'd started with earlier. However, the situation he was in didn't allow him to remain indecisive.

He kept walking. He still didn't know what was going on, though. He walked between tall tree trunks, trying to make out a trail.

He thought he glimpsed a dark figure jumping out of the bushes and vanishing again into the thick vegetation. He wasn't sure. He slowly turned his head, trying to see the figure. His gun swung in the same direction. And it was then that he realized that he was alone. No one was behind him. They had all disappeared.

His heart hammered like it was about to blow up. Panic took over and he made the worst mistake in his life.

"Where are you?" he shouted out, and suddenly realized that he wasn't alone at all.

A sudden, invisible force pushed against his chest and knocked him down, driving the wind out of him. When he recovered he realized that a great weight rested upon his stomach. He felt his skin being torn; he sensed his blood pouring out. He screamed. The last thing he saw before he fainted was a piece of his flesh hanging from the jaws of a strange animal.

He died just before three more predators attacked him, ripping off his arms and legs. The animals scattered quickly, running in different directions while the poor man's blood still dripped from their teeth.

He was the luckiest one.

The remaining soldier heard the leaves rustling in the passing breeze. He had drawn far away from the spot where he was earlier and had reached a clearing where he intended to contact the rest of the team by radio and tell them what had happened, if they were still alive. He looked around and saw nothing but a small trail leading into the tall trees surrounding him. Everything seemed normal.

He took the radio out and called one of the designated frequencies. At that same moment, he heard something moving behind the trees in front of him. He turned the radio off and crept toward the spot. He looked behind a big trunk and recoiled in horror when he saw the partially-dismembered body of one of his team mates. The body was in such a condition that he couldn't recognize who it had been.

Now he knew that the trees hid something very dangerous and threatening. He took a step backwards. He heard a second sound but couldn't tell where it came from. He quickly looked around but didn't see anything. He lifted the radio again and started to call, then stopped.

A strange looking animal stood in front of him-still, threatening, predatory.

He realized he was about to die, knew that the creature standing before him meant him harm, and had the power to do so.

He wouldn't die without a fight. He lifted his gun and aimed it at the creature but didn't pull the trigger.

Now he could clearly see that there were several animals and that they surrounded him. They didn't attack but merely stared at him with their cold eyes, seemingly weighing the situation.

The soldier studied them in return. Black stripes covered their dark green skin. Each of their arms ended in three hooked claws.

He stood, staring steadily at the animals, waiting for his end. But he would take one or more of those creatures with him. He aimed and prepared to fire.

He didn't make it. He felt a stab of pain in his back, immediately turned and faced a whole row of white spikes shining in the dark. It was a moment before he realized what he looked at.

The predator's teeth were the last image he saw before he lost consciousness.

The second team walked at a slow pace among the tree trunks. None of them could imagine what had happened to the other team, or what was about to happen to them.

The predators were already behind them.

The soldiers moved slowly in the dark, wearing special infrared goggles that made visibility only marginally better. One of them held a special device whose readings were visible in the infrared spectrum. A warning sound came from it. The soldier signaled the team leader to come closer.

"We've got a problem," the soldier holding the device whispered to the team leader. "According to this, two members of the other unit have no pulse, while the other three have unusual pulse rates and are all heading rapidly in the same direction!"

"Stay alert; you know these devices are hardly ever wrong," the commander said in a thoughtful voice.

The policemen manning the roadblocks outside the park heard the gunshots. None of them spoke. Frozen in their positions, they listened to the successive shots. The shots seemed to come from afar, but all of them knew that what they feared was actually very close.

The first unit was now scattered. Those who had managed to survive the sudden attack of the predators ran without knowing where they were going. Their only desire was to escape from what hunted them, to remain alive.

The captain panted with exhaustion but knew he shouldn't stop. He ran blindly with all the strength left in him. He careened against a tree and fell down. When he opened his eyes, all he could see in front of him was darkness.

Little by little he managed to make out, in the scant light, a face above him. He shuddered.

"John," he heard someone say.

He extended his hand for help standing up. "What happened to the rest?" he asked. The other didn't answer.

"We have to get out of here immediately," he said breathlessly. "These creatures don't die easily. I think I killed one. We'll come back tomorrow morning, in daylight, to see what it is."

"I've got few bullets left," the other soldier said, "but they're not enough to...John, are you listening to me?" "What's wrong?" At the same moment, he saw the captain's eyes. They stared at a spot behind him. There was something there, something the soldier couldn't see.

He wanted to turn his head and look. If these were to be his last moments, he wished at least to see what would kill him. He never had a chance. He saw the eyes of his friend and commander widen with surprise and terror, then felt the animal's teeth sink into his neck. He screamed with pain, but no sound came out, because he no longer had a voice.

It was the most horrible sight John had ever seen and it would be one of the last ones. He saw the other soldier fall to the ground, writhing. The animal stepped on him to hold him still. It leaned over him and, with a sudden jerk, finished off its victim.

Now it was busy with its prey. It glanced at the other man standing in front of it but then ignored him.

John knew well that even if he ran, he couldn't go much farther-not far enough to escape. He was being given another chance to escape, however. His fear held him in that position for a moment, but then fear also made him start running with all his strength.

But something told him the animal was on his trail.

The soldier's eyes opened little by little. He must have been unconscious for quite a while. He didn't know where he was or what had happened. He tried to remember but couldn't. He heard many jumbled sounds all around him, like twitters, but he couldn't see anything. It was some time before he realized he was in the midst of many tiny, watching eyes.

John was still running, hoping that somewhere ahead of him the park would end, giving way to the city streets. He hoped that if he managed to get there, the animal would stop stalking him. But he couldn't be sure. He had seen the predators' agility and speed, he had seen with his own eyes how they killed their prey. The one stalking him could catch him anytime, unless...unless it was playing with him.

That thought made him accelerate even more. He breathed rapidly, if one could call that breathing. His throat was dry. But his love of life forbade to him to stop and he would not stop.

The creature behind him knocked him down. He tumbled on the grass for a few feet and then stopped.

Some time had passed when he opened his eyes and realized where he was.

"Is that you, John?" he heard someone asking him. He sat up and looked around.

"What is this place?" he asked but didn't get an answer, at least not from the soldier. He could now clearly see that the tiny spots of light that had surrounded him weren't stars. They were the eyes of the predators, and they were looking him!

The numerous young predators came and went in the dark, seeming rather upset. The two men watched them without talking, waiting for the worst to happen. When they saw one of the animals approaching they didn't worry at all, because life for them had already reached the end.

The animal seemed to approach the two soldiers warily, at a slow but steady pace. It moved suddenly and John felt terrible pain as a large chunk of flesh was torn from his leg. He tried to hit the young predator but it ducked and ran away. Two other animals charged in and attacked and the two brave men screamed in pain, unable to defend themselves. And then a third and a fourth predator charged in...

John lay on the ground and as the predators attacked, he turned his head and managed to see, for the last time, the predators also attacking his team mate. In the next few minutes of terror and pain he wished only for a quick death. Even so, he realize what had happened. The larger animal had carried him and the other soldier to its den and delivered them to his brood. They were a hunting lesson. The moment of his death was the lesson learned.

ESCAPING!

"The mission unit is late to report, Mr. President. All life signs seem to have ceased."

Clive sat holding his chin and looking down at the floor, thinking.

"I guess we have to assume they're dead, right?" he said.

"They're definitely dead, Mr. President."

"Inform each one's family, provide compensation, but don't say they all died."

"Yes sir." The officer left.

"Now what? What do we do, Clive?" one of his advisors asked.

"Reinforce the roadblocks and arm three helicopters with napalm bombs. We'll wait for them to attack first."

"For Christ's sake, you know we mustn't-"

"I said, we'll wait." Clive looked at him strangely, almost regretfully. "You know there's nothing else we can do," he added, and everyone fell silent.

Morning light fell on the police cars that had been parked outside Central Park for the past five hours. The policemen and soldiers had lost their eagerness and moved listlessly from one vehicle to another. Some of them sat inside the cars, obviously upset. There was no traffic in the street where the roadblock had been set up. Half of Manhattan was deserted. All of them wanted to go home, to their families. They wanted to sleep, even for a little while, after such a wearying night. They waited impatiently for the order that would release them from duty.

One policeman sat in the front seat of his car, looking through the windshield at the others' movements. Every now and then, he moved his jaw up and down, chewing gum vigorously. No one was nearby to tell him to stop. A sharp crackling sound pierced the quiet, startling him. He immediately realized where the sound came from and lifted the radio microphone from the dashboard, pressing a button to activate it at the same time.

"I read you," he said, and stopped chewing the gum. "Yes sir," he said at one point, nodding. "Yes...yes sir," he said again. "At your order."

He changed frequencies and prepared to call another car and inform them that they must remain in position until further notice. He'd been told to transmit the order right away. But why didn't he? Why was he frozen behind the wheel?

He couldn't remember anymore what he'd been told to do. His eyes were searching, trying to detect again what they had noticed a moment earlier: a strange, dark green figure that popped out of the bushes and disappeared behind them again. He wasn't sure he'd seen it, but the chance that this wasn't a trick of his imagination was enough to make him shudder.

The policeman calmed himself by telling himself that such animals didn't exist. He grabbed the radio on his belt, opened the car door and stepped outside. As the door closed behind him, he wished he had never gotten out.

And death spreads
like tears from the Nile
like waves that rise
on the shadows of the Dream

Dozens of animals were jumping from among the trees and landing on the police cars. The car roofs buckled as the dark green creatures dropped on them. Startled policemen and soldiers ran, trying to escape. Those who remained and aimed their guns at the animals were very few. The predators didn't seem to care about the people.

Each one was as tall as an average man, with an upraised tail that whipped about dangerously, balancing the animal's movements. Their legs ended in deadly, sharp claws that made you believe there was nothing in this world that could stand up to them.

In a few seconds all of the creatures had scattered, leaving behind crushed vehicles and trampled people.

The policeman was left standing beside his car, watching awestruck as the last fleeing animal jumped from car to car, squeaking at the others as if begging them to wait for it. After a while, absolute quietness settled over the area.

SYDNEY

The room was dark. It was one of those few moments when the white walls absorbed the dark, thus attracting the attention of those locked inside them their whole lives. Every day gave them time to memorize every aspect of the world inside the walls, something those outside did not do. The black of night was a change, something different for the residents of the white rooms to appreciate.

Barry had set aside the book he was reading and now stared into one of the corners of the ceiling. The rest of his life would probably follow this pattern, but he didn't care. The four walls gave him something the outside world could not: safety. The terrifying experiences he had been through made him reassess the value of serenity and resolve to devote himself to it forever, and he'd succeeded-with the help of some cunning men. He hoped that one day he would be redeemed from the memories of the past, but the wound fear had left deep inside him still festered with a lust for revenge.

"Deinonychus, compsognathus, velociraptor…" Barry whispered, "it will come…"

The bed creaked as Barry stood up. He couldn't sleep. He walked to the window and rested his elbows on the narrow sill. Moonlight illuminated the courtyard and the high wall that separated him from the rest of the world. He looked nostalgically at the houses in the distance. It was quiet. Cars rarely passed through this neighborhood so late.

His eyes rose to look into the sky, at the thousands, millions of bright stars. It was an image truly heavenly, but at the same time impossibly distant. Seeing it was enough for him.

"Jimmy will be up there somewhere now," he said, giving voice to his thoughts. "We'll all go there soon."

His dropped his gaze to a part of the courtyard where trees, tall grass and flowers grew. Something had caught his attention. He stared at that spot for quite some time, trying to detect any more movement.

His patience rewarded him. He felt again the terror he had felt six years ago. The creatures still existed. The dinosaurs were still alive!

Shivers ran through his body. His face turned red with fear and vengefulness. And then he did something very unexpected. He smiled.

" 'Soon' is inappropriate," he said. " 'Today' is the right word." He moved silently back over to his bed and lay down.

THE RECOGNITION

The president moved from one office to another around the vast room, trying to oversee the government's actions as much as possible. Tension reddened his face, his stress was justified. Clive would be the first to be blamed in the event of failure. He would be the first man that the media would target-if there were any newspapers or television stations left, of course.

"Mr. President" somebody called from the other end of the room. "We have an event in Central Park."

"What do you mean?" Clive asked.

"Something very strange must have happened there, sir!"

"And that is...?"

"I talked to the chief of police a while ago; he was there."

"And what did he tell you?" Clive prompted.

"Half-truths, sir. I didn't get anything useful out of him!"

"But what could have happened, why didn't he tell you over the phone?" Clive asked. He was getting angry.

"What can I say, Mr. President?" the officer said in a low voice, as if he were the one at fault. "He sounded very agitated; he hung up on me. Something very strange is happening there and we don't know what, yet!"

"Wasn't there any videotaping, any television coverage?"

"You forbade television crews from crossing the blockade around the park."

"You don't have to remind me," Clive said, looking at him ruefully. Then he turned towards the Secretary of Defense. "Where are the helicopters with the napalm? We need them immediately!"

"I told you they'll be here in twenty to twenty-five minutes, maximum," the Defense Secretary responded in a tight voice. "Do you really intend to drop them in Central Park?"

"It looks like we may be too late…"

"Too late for what?" Foster asked.

"Don't be too anxious; we'll find out soon," Clive said without looking at him. "I'm sure that all the major channels have already picked up on the problem; I want to see what they're broadcasting and I want it now, god damn you!" Clive shouted, and slammed his hand on the desk next to him when no one complied immediately. "The news stations will have already informed the citizens of what's going on. This is big news for them; they have something to gain. Unlike the policemen, who reported to us merely because they were required to. But none of them dared to endanger their life simply out of duty."

"Yes sir," the officer manning a nearby computer said in a low voice that made Clive pause, "I'll connect you right away."

They all looked at the big screen. At that moment the doors burst open and a man walked in shouting the president's name. His was the only voice to be heard, and it quickly fell silent. Absolute silence fell over the room. No one spoke; they all stared at the images on the screen. What they saw immobilized everyone.

Clive stared at the screen in awe. He took a step forward without taking his eyes off the image. "What year is it?" he asked, but no one replied.

WHITE HOUSE

"This can't be happening; how can I be seeing, here and now, creatures that lived sixty-five million years ago?" the president asked desperately.

No one answered him. After a while, someone supplied, "Biotechnology. We can design and produce organisms. Someone did exactly that with these animals!"

Clive looked at him strangely and said nothing. But one thing was certain, he knew!

At that moment, three major cities-Sydney, New York and Buenos Aires-were under attack by the predators. This time the Jurassic scene was real.

OUTSIDE, IN THE CITY

Rivers of human blood, not cars, ran along the streets. Those unfortunates who hadn't escaped early from the city soon became the victims of the velociraptors. The dark green animals attacked everyone with no hesitation, without regret. They hunted out of instinct and a thirst for blood. The soldiers and policemen, unable to stop the creatures, soon suffered the same fate as the rest of the citizens.

A man's face, sweaty and wearing a terrified expression, peeked around the corner of a house. He looked quickly right and left, didn't see any danger, and mistakenly believed he was safe. He stooped and quickly lifted in his arms his six-year-old child. Behind them, the mother lay dead, torn in half.

The father covered his child's eyes and ran towards a car. He opened the door and got in, still holding the child tightly in his arms. Before turning the key in the ignition, he looked at the dead body of his wife for the last time. "I'll take care of him for you, I promise," he said, and his vision blurred with tears.

The car wouldn't start.

"Dad," the child said, "Dad, what's happened to you?"

The man had turned pale; he didn't say a word.

"Dad, why aren't you saying anything? Where is mum, dad?"

He held the child tightly in his arms; the little boy started to cry. At the same moment, a predator appeared only a hundred feet away. But he had promised her that he'd look after the boy, the man reminded himself; he couldn't break that promise.

He pulled a gun from his sweat-stained shirt and aimed. He had only one bullet, and the predator wasn't alone anymore. Four of them approached the car slowly, confident about their prey.

All hope was lost. But no, the man realized, the promise was still unbroken.

He looked his child in the eyes and whispered, crying, "I'm sorry..." He felt the boy's arms holding him; he felt the child's heart beating. He knew what he had to do. He caressed the little head and gently, as if he was handling the most valuable thing in the world, pulled the boy's head in front of his chest. He pulled the trigger. The bullet went through the child's head and lodged in the man's heart. They died together.

DANIEL & NANCY

The boy's heart beat quickly. He wanted to cry, to scream, but he knew that would cost him his life. Next to him, Nancy was motionless; you could only tell she was alive if you noticed her chest going up and down with her breathing. The two children knew they would end up dead.

Clara didn't know what to do. She knew she should set an example, but what kind of courage could she offer the two children when she herself couldn't overcome her fear?

"We'll all die," Nancy said. No one disagreed.

"We knew it from the beginning…we knew it," Daniel said.

Nancy looked at him with eyes full of reproach. "But we didn't do anything, Daniel. And that's exactly what we'll be punished for. We could be very far away now; we could have warned everyone, but we treated it like a game." She smiled bitterly. "Maybe grown-ups are right not to trust us after all."

"Don't say that again, Nancy," the boy said, "don't say it again."

"Why?"

"Because…because I read a book once; it was the only one I've ever read."

"Which book, Daniel?"

"A book…" tears filled his eyes, but those tears were not for the pain of the death that awaited them; no, those tears were for something else. ""It was a book about a prince. I remember it as if I'd read it yesterday!"

"I don't have any idea what you're talking about!" Nancy exclaimed.

"Then Nancy, you don't have any idea why you're alive, what you're waiting for!"

"It doesn't matter anymore," Nancy replied. "We'll be dead any moment now."

"No Nancy, if we die, if humanity is exterminated, that's exactly when that book and every book will really be worth something!"

The girl's mother broke in. "Stop talking about things like that, no one is going to die."

"Why haven't we got anything else left to us, mum?" Nancy asked, but didn't receive an answer.

"I'll tell you what we have to do," Daniel said with sudden confidence. "We have to fight; we must struggle. Humanity must not die, it doesn't deserve to die. I won't stay here with my hands tied. I will fight! I'll either win or be defeated, but I won't surrender. Just a while ago, I realized that-people don't deserve to die!"

There was a loud bang on the door. The velociraptors were trying to break it down. The boy's voice had acted like a beacon, telling them that someone was still alive.

Daniel and Nancy and Clara rose, seeking to escape, but the apartment building had become a prison. They had to find a way out, at any cost. The only door that led to the stairs and then to freedom was the one being battered by the predators. They couldn't jump from the third floor apartment. Time was running out; the door was beginning to buckle.

They were at a dead end!

With a metallic screech, the door tumbled to the floor. The predator's body tumbled inside with it, but the creature regained its feet in less than a second. It looked around and lifted its muzzle, scenting something disturbing. It moved forward slowly. Two more velociraptors came into sight behind it, smaller but no less dangerous. They strode forward together and moved to either side of the larger one.

Nancy, jammed in a closet with Daniel, watched the predators through the keyhole and hoped that they couldn't also sense her. One of the three got so close to their hiding place that it blocked the small hole. The girl closed her eyes and didn't move at all. She didn't want to know what was happening. When she opened her eyes again she saw a beam of light coming through the keyhole and falling upon her hand. The animal had moved.

She silently bent her head to look through the keyhole. At first she couldn't see anything, but then she was sure: no animal was out there-at least, not in the drawing room.

They would wait a bit longer and then they would have to leave before the fumes from the gas stove affected them. The thought of escape comforted her. She wished she could tell her mother they were going to be all right. "Maybe it wasn't so clever to separate after all," she thought, and turned her head to look at Daniel. Neither of them spoke.

"Give me a report on the situation," Clive said.

The officer sitting in front of the computer quickly typed a command, and moved the mouse on his desk. "Most people have fled from Manhattan; at least those who managed to get out of the dead zone. Those still inside are already dead or are doomed to die in the next few minutes. The predators have actually cleared the entire area around Central Park!"

"Now take into consideration the time that has elapsed since you received this information and you'll have two more blocks!" the president said as he worked out the figures on the computer screen.

"Mr. Clive" someone called from the other end of the room.

"I'm over here," he answered.

"The army is now crossing the Queensboro Bridge. They've set up roadblocks on all the other bridges to prevent the animals' escape."

"You mean the dinosaurs," Clive corrected.

"Dinosaurs are animals!"

"Very strong, fast, agile, animals; very clever. They differ from any species of our time except..."

"Except what?" Foster asked.

"Nothing...nothing. It's something completely insignificant," the president said."Except for us!" the officer at the computer suddenly exclaimed. "They resemble us! To look at them, you'd believe that nature followed a reversed evolutionary course!"

Clive looked irritated by this answer for a moment. "Evolution should be the last thing troubling us right now," he said, and punched a number into his cellular phone. "This is the President. I want double the military force that the Secretary of Defense asked for. I want them massed at the bridges into Manhattan. No, no, at both ends of the bridges. I also want a quarter of that force to enter the city to rescue as many citizens as possible, and to exterminate as many predators as they can. Rescue helicopters should fly at the proposed safe height and guide the infantry...Yes, yes, exactly. That's all" He hung up.

"I could object to that," the Secretary of Public Relations said. "Why should we reinforce the points where the animals could escape when we know that one third of the force already deployed is sufficient? We're leaving many people trapped in their homes, helpless."

"First of all, sir, we don't know what force will be necessary to prevent the escape of the animals. And secondly, by leaving those people, who are probably dead by now, we preserve the future of all the others. Life is valued, sir, not in money but in the cost of other lives. And I believe that it's preferable that a few, rather than many, die!"

The tension that possessed Nancy's body vanished as the danger passed. The velociraptors had given up hunting quite quickly, which seemed suspicious, but to the girl's mind, it simply implied safety.

The closed environment inside the closet bothered her, contrary to Daniel, who seemed to be relieved. She wanted to get out as soon as possible. She wished she knew how far away the predators were that hunted them. She also wondered briefly why they had given up their hunting so soon. She didn't want to think of anything negative; she was trying to be optimistic-an attitude usually beneficial, but which occasionally kills.

She lowered her eye to the keyhole again. Her movement made the clothes in the closet rustle slightly. She squinted, trying to focus properly, then sighed, obviously relieved.

"I can't see anything moving out there," she whispered. Daniel put his finger over his lips, signing to her to speak even more quietly. "Shall we get out?" she asked, but Daniel didn't speak. He looked as if he didn't know what they should do. They were both children, unable to count on the wisdom of their decisions. That's what they had been taught.

"No," he mumbled. "Let's stay here a little longer. It's so safe, so quiet."

"Are you sure?"

"What if we do go out; where will we go then?" he asked, but Nancy didn't have an answer.

Neither of them added anything more. They both sat wrapped in the soft, warm clothes.

They both grasped when they saw the closet door gradually opening.

Clive walked quickly towards the Secretary of Defense. "Where are they at this point?" he asked, turning to look at the large screen.

The sight there could not be ignored. A velociraptor jumped on a man in the middle of the street, knocking him down and ripping off his skin from shoulder to stomach in one motion. The creature left the man still alive and left to attack its next victim. The video image jolted a few times before it was replaced by snow.

"Did you hear what I said?" the Defense Secretary asked.

"What? No, I didn't hear. Could you repeat it, please?" the president said, perplexed by what he had just witnessed.

"The army is in place, Mr. President. They've blocked every escape route, every bridge leading to the other parts of New York."

"Perfect," Clive said. "We reacted quickly and correctly. Now we have time to get rid of those bastards."

"We have a small problem there," the Secretary said.

The president's expression changed. "What do you mean, 'a problem'?" he said ominously.

"I think we should discuss it alone, in your office, Mr. President."

The two withdrew, ostensibly to discuss the country's welfare, but the conversation actually centered on the two men's own interests.

Daniel and Nancy didn't move at all. They stared at the closet door as it opened. The light from without nearly blinded them, but they didn't close their eyes. They wanted to see, as long as they still could.

"There's no problem, children. Everything's fine, the animals have left," Clara said as she stepped from behind the closet door.

It took Daniel and Nancy a moment to realize what had happened.

"Mum," Nancy mumbled, "we were really scared, mum!"

"I know, honey; I was scared too!" Clara said, and took Nancy in her arms.

"They're gone now, aren't they?"

"They're far away now; I checked the house and turned off the gas before coming to get you out." Clara glanced at Daniel. He seemed exhausted and still upset, but relieved to still be alive. "Your idea to leave the gas on so the animals wouldn't be able to smell us worked, my boy!"

"Let's get out of here, now!" the boy stammered.

"It's hell down there, Daniel. We can't leave," Nancy told him. She pulled away from her mother and took a step out of the closet.

The house was a mess. The predators had ripped apart the couches and curtains. Nothing was where it was supposed to be. The floor was strewn with broken objects and the carpets were filthy. The light had been ripped from the ceiling. Everything was destroyed. The sight made Nancy realize how wild the creatures were.

"What happened in here mum?" Nancy asked.

"What you see, honey. They didn't leave anything intact, but it doesn't matter. We're alive. We can rebuild everything."

Nancy moved through the apartment to see what damaged had been done to the rest of it. Room after room displayed destruction that they'd almost became a part of. Nancy's eyes strayed to the television. It had fallen from the wall, but the screen seemed intact. There was a chance it could still function.

"Maybe we can find out what's going on out there with the TV!" Nancy said.

Her mother checked the TV set. "You're right, maybe television will show us a way to survive this nightmare. Maybe these animals-these dinosaurs, as you say they are-fear something that we don't know about. Or maybe there's a rescue operation underway and the information about where to go is being broadcast!"

Daniel clambered out of the closet. "Let's try it."

Clara bent over the TV. Nancy moved closer. She could feel broken things crunching under her feet and was afraid that an animal would hear her, but she didn't stop. She reached her mother and tried to help her prop the television upright on the floor while Daniel searched out the remote control in the mess.

Clara depressed the 'on' button. The forty inch screen didn't display anything but snow!

"Maybe it's damaged," Nancy suggested.

"I don't think so," Daniel said and approached the wall. "You know, most times the cable needs to be connected in order to watch television." He inserted the plug in the cable socket on the wall and immediately regretted that action.

The TV finally showed images, but it also emitted the words of·the reporter on the screen-sounds that would help the predators locate them.

The two kids nearly panicked at the loud noise. It had been several hours since they had heard a clear, loud voice. And they also realized that they had invited their enemy!

Daniel tried hastily to pull the TV's plug out. Nancy, crying desperately, pressed the 'off' button on the remote but missed it in her haste.

Daniel eventually managed to yank the cord from the socket. The sound from the television stopped, but it was replaced by another, more frightening sound: a twitter. They all froze, afraid to look for the source of the sound.

Nancy knew there was something in that room with them, something that wanted to hurt them. She wanted to cry, to scream. She could see her mother next to her, frightened, unable to move. Daniel was also frozen in place. They all knew that, unless they did something quickly, they wouldn't have time to come up with any better ideas.

The animal was really close by now. They all anticipated its attack. The longer it took to happen, the more terrifying the situation became.

Quite some time passed and the animal didn't attack. Daniel wondered if the predator had run away. No matter how irrational that thought seemed, it was his last and most fervent hope.

He wanted to look at Nancy and her mother behind him, to see how they were reacting. But, he reminded himself, if he moved and the predator was still there, he would be attacked. He couldn't just stand still, waiting for death to strike, because even if there was nothing behind them, there would be very soon.

It took a lot of courage for Daniel to look back. He gaped at what he saw.

There, in front of him, was a velociraptor-definitely dangerous, but hardly deadly, at its age!

The little predator, less than a foot tall, stood uncertainly and looked curiously at the three people who seemed more frightened of it, despite being larger and stronger, than it was of them.

Daniel scowled, realizing that they'd been worrying all this time about what a baby would do. "Let's get out of here!" he said.

Nancy and Clara, confused, turned to look too. The little dinosaur was staring at them.

"The big ones won't be long in coming!" Daniel urged, glancing around. "We must hurry!" Strange, he thought, but he felt more confident now, like he could count on himself!

"Are you sure it's not dangerous?" Clara asked.

Daniel gave her a side-long glance as answer. "Don't be afraid," he said, "it's still a baby."

The two kids walked slowly towards the front door. Despite their efforts, scattered debris on the floor broke under their feet every now and then. The boy moved past the small velociraptor, completely ignoring it. The baby turned its head to watch the boy drawing away. Nancy didn't take her eyes from the little creature as she passed it. Neither did Clara, who hesitated at first.

"Are you completely sure it's harmless, Daniel?" she asked.

Daniel looked back to discover that Nancy's mother was far behind them, still staring at the predator.

"It looks pretty wild to me!" Clara said.

"It'll do you no harm," Daniel assured her.

"Are you sure?"

"Positive!" he said and waved her forward.

Clara took a deep breath and moved slowly past the little dinosaur.

And then something completely unexpected happened!

The little velociraptor dashed toward the unsuspecting woman. Clara screamed as she felt the animal's small but sharp claws piercing her jeans and tearing the skin of her leg. The small green figure dropped to the floor and prepared to strike again.

Daniel didn't give it a second chance. He kicked it with all his strength and the predator flew into the air and slammed against the wall. It landed on the floor again, on its feet, seemingly intact.

"Completely harmless, right?" Clara said, pressing her hands over her bleeding leg. The boy wordlessly helped her stand up. They had to get away. The little one's parents would come soon and they wouldn't like what Daniel had done to their baby.

THE DECISION

"We have to decide upon two issues, gentlemen!" the president said, to the people around him. "I want to know, in particular, whether you agree to an air strike on Buenos Aires to eradicate the beasts there. I also want to know whether we should authorize the demolition of all the bridges leading to Manhattan."

One advisor spoke. "Mr. President, we know that the animals travel and reproduce in the subway tunnels, in tunnels they have created, and in other underground areas. Those on the surface are numerous, but they're much fewer than those hiding underground. Therefore, even an air strike would only kill a few of those creatures!"

"That no reason not to try. Besides, we know that velociraptors have high intelligence, so if we attack them on the surface, we might manage to drive them underground. That would give the land forces a chance to move in and trap them in their underground nests, where we will extinguish them!"

"What does the Argentinean government have to say about our plan?" someone asked.

"Their government has fallen. They're unable to find a solution and it's almost certain they'll accept whatever we have to offer."

"We could use Buenos Aires, of course…"

"As a testing ground. Absolutely. We'll see how the animals react to our war machines, with the least possible casualties of course, but it won't take place on American soil."

"We must make sure that this counterattack has as many variations as possible, to determine which course will be most effective."

"No, I talked it over with the Secretary of Defense a while ago, and the strike should be made only by air."

"That deprives us of many advantages."

"But it also exonerates us from meaningless deaths. Besides, NATO will probably organize the operation, and they've declared on behalf of four powerful European countries that they are not going to send any ground troops."

"What are the specific targets going to be?"

"Anything moving," the president replied firmly, "as well as large buildings whose basements likely hold colonies of predators."

"What about the innocent citizens? Some of them will become victims of our missiles!" another advisor protested.

"There will be very few casualties, and no one will ever learn who their real executioner was."

"All right, I have no objection," the advisor conceded. "It seems like it's our only solution."

"What about the rest of you? Do you agree, yes or no?" Clive asked the council. They all raised their hands in approval.

"Well, now, as far as the other issue is concerned, blowing up the **bridges is the only solution. We're very lucky that Manhattan is a big island. We have the opportunity to block their escape and exterminate them completely!**"

"Have you considered what that would mean, Mr. President?" Foster objected. "If we blow up the bridges, we'll have cut off every route to the rest of the city. The ground troops will be able to approach the stricken area only by ship and aircraft, while the survivors will be unable to escape."

"Sir, I don't think you got my point. I didn't say I would withdraw all the forces that are already in the city; we're not going to leave anyone without help. Besides, by isolating Manhattan, we contain not just the people but the velociraptors as well."

"Yes, but don't you think you could-"

"There won't be any further discussion of this issue; it's a decision the Senate and I agree to. This matter is resolved!" Clive announced, and in doing so condemned some people, saved others, committed political suicide and remained alive!

THE CAMP

The sun was rising on the horizon of the vast plain to the right of the airport. Its light touched on the pilots waiting on the parade ground and cast their shadows behind them in sharp silhouettes. The morning breeze made the flag ripple, the only moving thing. The sound of a door opening added life to the entirely motionless scene. A man, dressed differently than all the rest, walked quickly to the reviewing stand and climbed the stairs. Feedback came out of the speakers in every corner of the camp before the microphone picked up and conveyed the man's words.

"I'm sure that you, just like me, know what we were mobilized for. A day has already passed since we were informed of the first attack of those bloodthirsty animals. We're here to prevent anyone from having to repeat these same words tomorrow. We're here to prevent those vicious creatures from killing any more people, and from bringing again tears to the eyes of those who survived. In a few words, soldiers, we're here to stop, kill and eliminate those overgrown lizardsonce again from the face of the earth. Because there's no doubt anymore. If those creatures are not dinosaurs, then they're a life form that mimics dinosaurs!

"Many of you must be wondering how the hell those animals managed to survive, or even be reborn. That's something we don't know yet, but we'll make sure we find out right after their elimination. That's why I don't want any of you to dare tell me he missed even one of them! This time we have to be perfect and leave nothing undone.

"I've already received direct orders from the President. We're forbidden to destroy the whole of Manhattan; too many helpless lives would be lost to our own missiles. The only thing we have to do is aim and fire directly at the enemy, and only at the enemy, which is not at all helpless.

"The predators' speed is almost inconceivable. If an animal wishes to kill you it will have no difficulty in doing so. There is a lot more you must learn, that's why there are seminars you must take before the mission commences.

"I'm not here simply to inform you of the powers and weaknesses of the predators, but also to light a fire inside you. I'm sure many of you remember past actions, when you fought against other men. Enemies, hostile, but always other men! You're all Americans willing to sacrifice themselves for their country, without being asked to do so. The soil you're standing on right now is your country. But remember this; the soil is the same everywhere, and the man standing on it is neither American nor European, but a man who would never set boundaries; not in his mind or in his world. And if you were to die for your country, consider this: what sacrifice could be enough for a man's country?

"We once fought to gain more land, more rights. Today we'll fight for a single right. Today all people share a common enemy, and it's the first time in history that all people are united! Soldiers, you have no right to miss your targets. I'll be expecting absolute success of your mission."

His speech managed to fire the morale of the pilots gathered in front of him. Their eyes looked to the horizon, as if seeking a ray of hope. But there was nothing. The whole of Manhattan, in addition to Sydney and Buenos Aires, had been brought low by the predators' attacks.

Up to that point, the events were merely incidents…

The rows of pilots standing at attention scattered. Some withdrew to briefings covering final details; others inspected aircraft; nobody was idle. Time was short, but the price was high; there could be no time for rest. The whole camp had acquired a kind of urgency.

DAILY NEWSPAPER TITLES

1-What for?
2-Tears take time, time doesn't exist!
3-What kind?
4-When the past meets the present…
5-The End

1-What for?

Humanity's occupation of earth has been limited to a few thousand years. And I use the word "limited" because the duration of our existence seems minimal compared to the billions of years that earth has existed. We have, however, managed to change the face of the earth as no one else has. We have managed to replace its forests with buildings, its soil with coal tar. We must be really proud of this "revolutionary" ability of ours, which also happens to be self-destructive. We're not the only ones who pay for our mistakes; every other living organism on this planet does so, as well. They have no other option.

However, nothing in this world remains inert when it's in danger; everything defends itself, and the reappearance of creatures that lived seventy-five million years ago is nothing more than nature defending itself from the greed of humanity. The same mother that gave birth to us is now trying to destroy us; that's how unworthy we've proven to be!

Despite that, every mother is ready to forgive her child, even at the last minute. It's up to us. The predators have now spread everywhere, killing everything alive in their path, within Manhattan and without. They will continue advancing as long as we all fail to recognize the mistakes of the past. Our fate is in our hands, and we must act according to our thoughts and feelings. Try to see this truth. Humanity has always had the upper hand, we have dominated the planet and never feared losing that power; at least, not until today. Let's accept that we abused the power we had, and in that moment of realization, we will feel inferior, defeated. Humanity will not regain its ascendancy until the moment those animals die for the second time in history!

All of us hope for this miracle, because if humanity really wanted the world to survive, we would kill ourselves first! If humanity's glory was truly great, we would not be so naturally destructive!

TV-SYDNEY NEWS

"Four days ago, the whole world had the opportunity to observe a horrible sight. Predators literally destroyed the city of Sydney, leaving thousands dead and millions terrified.

As you know, these destructive creatures haven't victimized our city alone but two more cities, as well. What you might not know yet is that the velociraptors, as they have been identified by paleontologists, are leaving their nests in the center of Sydney and advancing outward, in groups and individually. It's estimated that, four hours from now, they'll have reached the outskirts of the city.

According to the last information we have, a great military force is gathering there to meet the creatures. Military spokespersons are optimistic; however, no one will take responsibility to tell us whether the armed forces are more powerful than the enemy.

The exact number of predators is very difficult to ascertain or even approximate, because the creatures most often move underground, through the subway tunnels. We can only wait four more hours, until the fight between the armed forces and the velociraptors takes place.

But, is waiting the right solution? In this case, definitely not. Every passing minute demands that we to do something so that it won't be our last. The velociraptors have taken advantage of our lack of vigilance, and now they number in the hundreds!

The first estimations were of about 140 adult predators. That number doesn't include the offspring, which are difficult to spot. Their high reproductive rate is one of their biggest advantages. This, coupled with amazing speed and intelligence superior to that of apes, enables successful perpetuation of the species. We know that velociraptor eggs hatch in less than three days!

Rough calculations and present conditions suggest that velociraptors could spread over all Australia in eight days. Things are much worse than they seem, but there's one thing we must avoid, and that's panic. Many people have already left, or are preparing to leave, their town and even the country, with Europe being their ultimate destination. This is considered feasible only on the west side of our continent. To prevent the species' spread, thorough checks are made on every flight, which slows transportation down.

Tickets are free and offered first-come-first-serve, but they are extremely scarce, unavailable even on the black market. Until you are able to evacuate, move as far west as possible. Luggage is not allowed. Anyone wishing to leave on a ship is being denied because no ships have permission to sail. A thorough check of ships is impossible. Private planes and sea vessels are also being denied departure."

DEPARTURE BY SEA
TO FOREIGN TERRITORY
IS PROHIBITED

The sign on the beach was blocked by thick vegetation and difficult to see. Sea salt had also left encrustations on the sign.

Some people, however, just didn't realize the implication of the rusty letters.

"The weather is wonderful," Jerry said as he walked slowly along the sandy beach.

"We're lucky, my friend; we've avoided the suffering, we'll escape," Angela, following him, said.

Both paused for a while to look out at the vast ocean.

"Do you think we can make it?"

"I'm sure. Besides, it's better than waiting ten days until our turn comes up. The way to New Guinea is open and in front of us." Jerry pointed expansively at the sea.

"I don't know, Jerry. If this is the only sure way out, then how come no one else is using it? As you can see, we're here by ourselves!"

"I knew from the beginning that you'd be giving orders. You have to understand that it's not the most rational way, but it's the one that will lead us to safety. Jesus Christ! Don't you want to live? It's no big deal if we break a few rules. Besides, the rules were made to make our life easier so it's right to sacrifice them in order to protect it." Jerry suddenly stopped, feeling ice-cold ocean water on his foot. A small wave broke over the young man's shoes.

"We've lost a lot of time," he said, "they said about four hours, on television. How long has it been since then?" He glanced at his watch, then ran towards their car, parked back from the ocean.

"We're late," he shouted. "Come quickly to the car with me; I have the portable TV there!"

TV

"...the picture you see is directly from the Sydney district where thousands of soldiers have been called up to prevent the predators from escaping. However, possibility turned into probability in these past few hours, when a significant transfer of the animals' population was observed. The velociraptors are obviously not satisfied with the destruction of such a large city. Their aim now is to move even farther out. The guns, tanks and soldiers-the entire picture you see before your eyes-might be our last hope to confront this evil before it spreads. If the velociraptors manage to break through this gigantic blockade, they'll be able to do anything. If these soldiers lose the battle, then the future of humanity will be uncertain. They have to stop them!"

The television broadcast silent scenes that cast doubt upon whether the area was really as quiet as it seemed. Then something happened that demonstrated to all viewers in the world that nothing was as quiet as it seemed.

It was now certain that attack was imminent upon the gigantic blockade that had been set up on at the city's outskirts. Every soldier took his position and the tanks' engines were started. Tension showed on the soldiers' faces; they were all alert. The world waited with them. The moment of truth had arrived.

Everyone looked to the city. The densely-packed buildings were a great distance from them, thus increasing the demand on troops and at the same time giving the soldiers ample time to intercept the predators without getting dangerously close. Watchers high on tall buildings, equipped with every kind of detection device, waited tensely for the enemy to appear.

One of those watchers saw the first predator running relentlessly towards them. At the same moment, he realized that other velociraptors followed. It was a massive break-out!

The soldier's reaction was immediate but not faster than the predators that had already entered the range of the infantry's guns. The sound of the guns firing announced the enemy's appearance. Dozens of ground-to-ground missiles were being launched, killing few or no velociraptors. The machine guns were too far away to do more than injure the agile animals. However, none of the soldiers retreated, even though the distance between them and the enemy was constantly decreasing and the number of velociraptors seemed endless.

The same situation existed all around Sydney, at every part of the blockade, since the predators' escape was attempted simultaneously. The behavior of the animals indicated astonishing organizational skills that indicated intelligence!

"No one can describe what we're now watching, ladies and gentlemen, no one can describe our feelings. It's obvious that we underestimated the number and power of these animals. We can now see them gradually approaching us. The broadcast will continue automatically. God help us all!"

The first predator was already three hundred feet from the blockade. There were only a few seconds left before it arrived, unless someone stopped it. Everyone's attention concentrated on it. The animal dropped, growling and rolling with the momentum of its great speed, while a cloud of gun smoke billowed from the ammunition that had struck that spot. The soldiers soon realized what a big mistake they had made.

Three velociraptors jumped almost simultaneously from within the cloud. The time the soldiers had wasted to exterminate the first predator proved fatal. Very soon two of the animals were passing through the vehicles and the people without hurting anyone, as if they merely sought to escape. Some soldiers froze in amazement. Soon more and more velociraptors were amongst them, and then beyond them, free. In a minute, all the adult animals had managed to get out of the city, leaving behind a cloud of dust and wonder.

Some of the soldiers stood and looked at the great numbers of predators running in groups away from the city. Few gunshots were heard, only the thunder of the animals' footsteps filled the air.

One of the soldiers wondered why the velociraptors, already half a mile away, didn't attack the people. They definitely outnumbered the people and were more powerful. Why did they all attack all over the district instead of gathering and striking at one point? Maybe velociraptors were quick and agile, but, as this action showed, also stupid after all! That thought reassured him and gave him a reason to keep hoping. This defeat wasn't a total, worldwide defeat.

Many of the soldiers had stood up, watching perplexed as the predators gradually disappeared over the horizon. Everything was over and the battle's outcome was thousands of free velociraptors and two human casualties. But something was wrong with the last one. Nobody knew why, but they all felt that the number of reported victims was much too few.

This was going to be corrected very soon!

The soldiers now watched in horror as the animals reformed and turned back to those they had left alive. Human voices and screams of fear filled the air. They watched the animals approaching, unable to do anything. There was confusion and the chaos. The velociraptors were already so close that the soldiers could make their eyes out. Now the predators had a different look. They were more aggressive; their only desire was to darken the light in the people's eyes.

Some soldiers just waited, others chose to fight till the end. However, they all felt the same pain, they died at the same moment. The attack came from behind them. Only half the predators had left in the first wave, while the rest stayed in the city, ready to surround and extermi-nate the whole blockade.

Not long after, the television displayed on the screen: human casual-ties 2,000,000.

That tallied the bodies, the torn and bleeding faces. But for us it would be something more than that...

WE'RE LEAVING RIGHT NOW!

Jerry and Angela watched the small screen, horrified. Escape was the most logical choice, if not the solution to the problem.

"Let's get out of here now," Angela said, without removing her eyes from the screen. "Let's leave this damned place right now."

Jerry nodded. They took everything they could from the car and carried it quickly to the boat. In a few minutes they were ready to sail.

"I'll really miss Australia," Jerry said, looking at the land bleakly.

"Come on, you're not leaving it forever," Angela replied, casting off the rope that tied the boat to the shore.

"I don't know why, but it seems to me like I'm seeing it for the last time before these creatures spoil it."

The sound of the engine covered Jerry's words. He was the only one who had heard them. That thought came and left just as the vessel left Australia at that point to end up at another.

AIRCRAFTS IN BUENOS AIRES

The NATO air strike force flew to Buenos Aires determined to strike the predators and kill as many as possible. It was going to be a fight that, for the first time in history, would be fought by humanity for humanity!

The city's first tall buildings were visible on the horizon. In a few seconds, the aircraft had reduced their altitude and assumed attack formation. The bombing of the area was next!

The first combat aircraft turned right and dived; two more followed behind it. Flying almost level with the buildings, the aircraft with the code name Hawk Two decreased its speed. The pilot concentrated on detecting a predator. It didn't take long to locate one.

He saw a dark green figure running unbelievably fast along a wide street. It moved in the same direction as the plane, about three hundred feet ahead.

"You're free to fire," a voice said through the radio. The screen displayed the characteristic message *Locked*. The only thing left was to fire the missile and the first animal would be history.

"Hawk Two, missile one. Fire," the pilot confirmed and everyone silently watched the first missile approach the predator. Seconds seemed like centuries.

The velociraptor stopped running, turned its head slowly back, and faced the human weapon coming towards it. Its eyes shone but it didn't move, as if it knew it couldn't run away from its fate. The explosion that followed was accompanied by smiles, sighs of relief, and laughter from the people who watched the scene unfold. Things didn't seem so bad. Humanity could still hope to regain the right to normal life.

"Order green light for the continuation of the operation," the Secretary of Defense said from the War Room. At the same moment, all the aircraft dived on the city, each with its own target, on its own mission. Chaos followed as buildings were demolished and the streets rocked with explosions.

The predators ran, panicked, seeming unable to face the human counterattack. Those watching the whole scene felt a sense of safety and confidence. It was fact: man had imposed his superiority over nature with the force of his weapons. But can the infant be more powerful its mother? Definitely not!

In the War Room the atmosphere was cheerful. They all believed that the problem had been solved and that it was simply a matter of time before that new form of life was controlled and exterminated. Everyone smiled at that first victory. Only one man sat staring perplexed at the screen without sharing in the others' joy, and what he was watching was worth everybody's attention.

A velociraptor held its position while a missile headed directly towards it. There was an explosion as the missile hit its target, but the predator was no longer there! They were faster than anyone had imagined, and they had the intelligence to take advantage of their speed. The first animal had indeed died. The others learned from its mistake and developed a technique to avoid the explosions. Within a minute there was only one death in every twenty missiles. Time and weaponry were insufficient to defeat the animals. The order was given to cease firing on the living targets and concentrate on destroying the buildings known to be occupied by predators. There seemed to be no obstacle to achieving that objective, at least, no obstacle that could be foreseen...

Two of the NATO aircraft were already in firing range. They only had to press a button and the building would blow sky-high. But they didn't; they flew over them, hesitating to kill not the predators, but five human children, five innocent souls. The velociraptors knew that weakness very well; they kept hostages. Whether that was instinctive or learned was uncertain, but they were taking advantage of human weakness to gain the upper hand. The hostages, all little children, were on the rooftop of a building colonized by the creatures. Two velociraptors guarded them and kept them in each corner of the roof to prevent the pilots from destroying that building with a clear conscience.

That wasn't the only building. There were two more in that city and God knows how many more in the other two cities. The result was the same everywhere. No one would destroy the buildings they protected, even if those children were destined to die later!

The aircraft drew away from Buenos Aires one after the other. Nobody knew what to do, but they all knew one thing: they had lost. The battle ended, adding one more defeat to the last pages of the book called "Humanity"-a book that could have become even bigger if man hadn't been so greedy, so selfish.

Hunting Children…

Daniel, Nancy, and Clara had abandoned their home. The woman limped, favoring the wound inflicted by the little predator on her left leg. The pain wasn't enough to make her stop, not when faced with the hope of finding a rescue unit or at least some survivors. But above all, she needed to instill a sense of solidarity. Who had the confidence at such moments to instill it in the others, too? Clara wasn't the one who needed help. All of humanity needed it, as it gradually fell into the well of obscurity without finding anyone to hold onto.

Nancy, exhausted by both exertion and strain, stopped walking. She sat down in the street and held her knees. Her mother and Daniel sat next to Nancy without complaint, since they were just as tired.

"Well, what do you know," the little girl said. "All these streets were once filled with cars going up and down like crazy and with living people, some smiling, others sad."

"That's how it used to be but…not anymore," Daniel said. "Today there's not a single soul in the streets. Dead people can't laugh or cry. They're all silent."

They heard a scream in the distance. Maybe at that moment one more person was dying, but that wasn't important to anyone anymore. Millions of people had died in the last few hours and no one knew how long it would go on.

"Don't look," Nancy's mother said. "It's very cruel and it's not proper for you to see." She turned her head in another direction. But the same horrible scene was everywhere. They couldn't avoid the horrors, which would never be completely eradicated from those children's minds.

"Whose fault is all this?" Nancy asked and laid her head on her mother's shoulder, seeking some comfort.

"I don't know, sweetie," Clara said, looking vacantly at the destruction around them. Her eyes were filled with misery and despair. "Man, I...I suppose, but I'm not sure." She tried to hide her feelings of hopelessness from the kids, so they wouldn't be scared.

"There must be someone to blame, mum," Nancy said, "you've never scolded me when I haven't done anything wrong."

Nancy's mother listened to her daughter's words and wondered whether the thoughts of a child, thoughts that had been formed by scenes of destruction and feelings of ignorance and innocence, were a part of reality after all. She wished it wasn't so, but she knew it was true.

"What have we done, who's punishing us?" Nancy wondered. No one answered, but not because the question didn't have an answer.

Daniel had noticed the presence of two creatures a few feet away from them. They were velociraptors, and they'd been watching the three humans for quite some time.

They had lost sight of land. The only thing they could see was the setting sun on a blue horizon. The sea was unusually calm. There was a breeze so slight, it barely existed. It was a scene one could really enjoy, but not the two young people now sailing these waters. They knew that at the same moment they were leaving their homeland, a friend or acquaintance was suffering.

The sun dropped below the horizon. Night gradually fell, spreading darkness across the sky, making everything glow that had earlier been lost in the sun's light. Jerry and Angela had to prepare before the darkness obstructed them. They would take turns keeping half-night watches, giving the other the opportunity to rest.

"Are you sure you won't fall asleep?" Angela asked.

"Don't worry, I'm used to taking responsibility."

"What kind of responsibility are you talking about, when one mistake from you could cost our lives?"

"For Christ's sake!" Jerry exclaimed, "what could happen to us where we are now?"

"Maybe you're right. I don't know why, but I can't calm down."

"You've been like that since the beginning of the trip. Stop it and try to relax"

"I will," Angela assured him.

"Great. And remember, as long as I'm awake there's nothing to be afraid of," he said and lit the gas lamp.

They said goodnight and withdrew to their positions. The sea reflected the rising moon.

Not more than two hours later, a sudden and unusual sound caught Jerry's attention. He quickly turned his head but didn't see anything. He peered into the darkness.

"Is there anybody there?"

No answer.

Maybe it was a bird that had flown far away from land, he thought. He grabbed the soft drink he'd been drinking and threw the can forcefully toward the spot where the sound had come from. No response. It was probably all in his imagination. Everything that had happened over the last few days had affected his mind, making him hear sounds that didn't exist.

At least, that's what he thought...

Nancy's breath caught as she lifted her head and saw the two velociraptors standing about eighty feet away, finishing off what was left of a man. Clara grabbed the two children by the hands and stood up, terrified.

The eyes of the two predators followed her movements. They abandoned their last victim and started walking towards them. They didn't hurry.

Their prey ran towards the nearest building, their only way to escape.

Clara pushed hard on the sliding door, pulling her daughter inside with her. Daniel followed without looking back. They entered a large foyer with many doors opening off it. A staircase rose in front of them, leading to another mezzanine with the same number of doors.

They couldn't decide where to go, but they knew they didn't have much time to think about it. The creaking of the door behind them reminded them of the hunters' presence. Every second counted.

Several minutes had passed since Jerry had heard that strange sound. That odd twitter stuck in his mind, troubling him and filling him with fear and doubt. He tried to think of something else, to take his mind off the horrifying scenes his imagination conjured.

He stood up and moved slowly to the vessel's prow. He bent and looked at the black sea that shone under the moonlight. He heard waves breaking on each other, and the serene sound of the water calmed down every wild instinct and soothed his frightened soul.

A twitter rose above the sound of the waves, followed by a scream louder than the voice of the sea. Then silence, as a last wave washed away the blood into the ocean...

One of them was dead, the other would die soon, but the vessel hadn't stopped floating. The waves and the wind would carry it while the flesh of the two young people would sustain the life form on board for as long as necessary.

They had reached the top of the stairs. Clara looked back to see how far away the predators were. She realized, horrified, that one of them was already inside and was hesitantly climbing the stairs.

She grabbed her daughter and ran to the nearest door, while Daniel followed behind. Bad luck; it was locked. She tried opening the neighboring one with shaky hands.

For a moment they had believed they could be lucky, but they soon realized they were at a dead end. In the meantime, the predator was topping the stairs.

Cold sweat beaded on Clara's face. She couldn't accept the fact that she would die up here, unable to help the two children.

Everything indicated that their lives would soon end. The first velociraptor slowly stepped onto the last step, eyes never leaving its prey. It waited for the second animal to arrive before they both approached the three people.

Nancy sobbed; she hugged her mother and screamed, "I don't want to die!"

The predators kept approaching, then stopped. Almost simultaneously, they crouched. Nancy covered her eyes. Everything seemed to stop. The seconds seemed like hours.

But death did not come. Clara opened her eyes, fearfully facing the predators' attack. To her great surprise, the velociraptors weren't there anymore. It didn't seem logical, but no one wanted to explain it. The only thing certain was that it was the best thing that could have happened.

Unfortunately, it was going to get worse…

THE BRIDGES

The air strike force sent to demolish every bridge that led to Manhattan had reached its target. The fighters dropped their altitude and prepared to fire.

"Do we have permission to fire?" the squadron commander asked. The answer was up to the president alone.

"You have it," Clive said.

At that moment, the missiles immediately shot toward every bridge. The pilots didn't question whether what they did was right, they only followed orders.

Successive explosions were heard. Manhattan, and everything within it, had been isolated from the mainland!

DEINONYCHUS

The sound of the explosions rocked Manhattan. The predators didn't appear concerned, nor did they attempt to attack those destroying the bridges.

"What are those sounds, mum?" Nancy asked.

"Aircraft. They're probably here to help us," Clara said but didn't say any more. For some reason, Daniel had signed to her to hush, but why?

It didn't take her long to realize what had frightened Daniel. A gray-hued figure was looking at them, apparently as surprised as they were. It looked similar to the other animals, but it wasn't identical. It was smaller and its skin was a different color of gray. Like the velociraptors, its legs ended in long, sharp claws. It didn't seem any more ferocious than the other predators, but nevertheless, it had just put two velociraptors to flight!

It was a deinonychus. Its eyes glowed with satisfaction over the three live victims it had discovered. Without pausing for thought, it jumped onto the staircase and from there directly to the upper floor.

Nancy screamed in terror and grasped her mother's hand. The deinonychus took two steps forward, lifting its tail and lowering its head. It charged, approaching at incredible speed.

A gunshot rang out. The animal tumbled onto Clara, thrusting her back several feet, but its lethal claws did not strike her. She fell, more terrified than hurt.

Daniel clutched the gun he'd taken from the dead policeman lying beside him and stared at the bullet hole in the animal's chest as the predator began jolting spasmodically. Its blood pooled in a huge circle around it. The deinonychus stopped moving. Only the tip of its tail continued twitching for a few seconds. The animal was dead; the danger had passed. At least, until the rest of the predators smelled the blood spreading over the floor and came to take their share!

SOMETHING TO LIVE FOR...

As if it was the lily
in the light of a sunbeam
lost hope
forgotten life
of my dream dripping
a love, a sorrow
but her tear
will drown the seas!

THE ROOT OF THE PROBLEM!

"The last bridge was taken out a second ago, sir," an officer reported.

Clive, expressionless, withdrew from the room, signing for the Secretary of Defense to follow him. They entered a small room containing only two desks and closed the door.

"Listen carefully," the president murmured. "You and I know very well where these animals come from; I'm sure I don't have to remind you."

"Of course not."

"You make it sound very simple. It's not enough that we knew about the program before it turned into a problem. There must be some records or papers that will reveal how these animals can be defeated. There must be some solution, except we don't have it right now!"

"What are you getting at?"

"Listen, there's no other way to stop this. The only thing left is to find the program's records. Those animals were designed by us, even if peripherally; therefore, there must be a weakness, or some kind of safety measure built into them."

"Clive, you haven't got any idea what you're saying right now. You can't find information on the program except from the laboratories that produced the animals. You remember the Amazon incident, of course; it cost us a lot to bury it..."

"It's the only solution that's left. I want you to organize a team of the best for a top secret mission. I want them ready to infiltrate the 'farm' in two hours."

"With what justification Clive? What orders do I give them?"

"Make a map and show them where the center is. I know there's an electric substation there that could be operated, but they'll have to get it working first. From there, they can connect to the local network with one of our satellites and upload all the records on the hard disks."

"For Christ's sake, Clive, have you considered what you're about to do, what consequences this will have for us? It will be obvious that we were involved with the biological weapons development program, that the construction and maintenance of the 'farm' was our work. We'll be held responsible for everything that has happened so far and we'll probably be convicted as war criminals!"

The president's look had changed; he didn't seem to care for himself. "I've regretted the decisions I made then a thousand times in the past few days," he said. "If I'm to continue living, I don't want to regret my decisions again."

"Is that all?" the Secretary asked sardonically.

"Not all. In case you haven't realized, we're accomplices in the horrible murders of millions of people. Something like that can't be left unpunished!"

The Secretary nodded, obviously regretting his earlier attitude. "I can't do otherwise; whatever you say, we're both doomed," he said. "But, you should now this mission will be suicide!"

In less than two hours the soldiers had been called up, instruction had been given and the mission was ready to set off.

THE "FARM"

The setting sun's light shone red on the Amazon jungle. Many things had changed in the last days; man's future seemed uncertain and history seemed to have altered its usual course. Tomorrow seemed like a dream, while today being alive was a luxury compared to the millions of lost lives. The sun's light was the only thing that remained eternal, after all.

A black helicopter flew in front of the sun, its gray shadow covering a part of the ocean of trees that lay below it. The shadow grew bigger as the helicopter gradually approached the ground. It stopped above a clearing, kicking up green waves on the sward. A ladder was thrown out of it and twelve men came quickly down the ladder. In a few seconds a whole unit of the Special Forces stood alone in one of the biggest jungles in the world.

Of course "all alone" was completely relative…

"I want you all ready in forty seconds," the commander said, pointing at a big box sitting next to him. In less than the prescribed time, every soldier stood equipped with the weaponry appropriate to his specialty. The leader signaled to two team members to take the lead.

The leaves of the trees rubbed against the soldiers' uniforms but they didn't care. They had to be constantly alert, since even the slightest mistake could prove fatal for them and for all people. Maybe that was the

reason why cold sweat trickled down their faces as they watched the setting sun deprive them of one more advantage: the safety of daylight.

They were walking through the dense vegetation but they moved like
they knew the road they followed well. The road was the last thing they
had to worry about. As they knew better than anyone, the Amazon did-
n't just host panthers and other dangerous cats, but also a new species, a
new form of life that looked more like reptiles but didn't belong anywhere, not even in our times!

They had already advanced deep into the jungle. Now, wherever one
looked he would only see the same huge plants and trees rising in front
of him, like tall towers in a beautiful, unusual city. The dense vegetation
cut visibility but since when did humanity learn to see far? Today, the
jungle was man's enemy, despite the fact that it had been his initial
home. The predators had already targeted the men, who hadn't understood anything!

The first soldier in the line signaled those behind to stop. He bent
and smoothly brushed aside a large green leaf in front of him with the
barrel of his gun. A wall about six feet high rose in front of him, painted
in camouflage colors. It was obvious that this building was meant to
stay secret and remain far away from the indiscreet eyes of the rest of
the world.

The soldiers immediately surrounded the small square building. One
of them signaled the others to join him. He had found the entry into the
small building.That part of the wall seemed like it had been shifted
from its position, but on closer inspection, they recognized a camou-
flaged door, which had been vandalized. Whoever had damaged it had
definitely pried at it using blades and a lot of strength-or perhaps the
hooked claws of predators. But, whatever had happened here had happened long ago; the vegetation had overgrown it, and both spiders and
rust had settled in.

One thing was sure. That door hid a well-buried secret behind it, a secret that after all those years was ready to emerge and convulse the world.

"Cover me," the leader said and, turning on the lamp on his helmet, stepped into the opening. His spotlight revealed a ladder that led downwards, into the earth. He turned off the light and put on his infrared goggles.

The ladder was wide; it disappeared into the darkness of the shaft. The walls seemed intact, despite the passage of time. A huge ventilation pipe hung over the ladder. There were some electrical boards on the wall, but nothing seemed to work. That was all the soldier could see due in the bad lighting.

There was also something else in there that he couldn't see, but it made him shudder: a strange, very heavy odor of rotten flesh. He hoped it wasn't human.

He clambered three steps down the ladder and signaled the rest to follow him. They entered one by one, wearing gas masks to avoid the stench. They quickly descended, reaching a small, square room with a wall that seemed to be a huge mirror. Like the door, it had been broken at some point, and now an adult human and of course a velociraptor- could pass through the opening.

The soldiers pressed their backs to the wall, weapons ready; some of them aimed at the hole in the mirror. The leader took a card out of a pocket in his backpack and then turned to scan the wall on the right side of the room. There was another electrical board there. This one seemed to be intact; perhaps it was even marginally operational.

Confident of what he should do, the commander took a deep breath and inserted the card in one of the board's slots, then typed in *POW/man*. An indicator light that had initially shone red turned to green, and the soldier released his breath, relieved, at the same instant. He grabbed a large lever and moved it up and down twice. And then, everything changed...

No one could ever have imagined what that place looked like when illuminated. Everything indicated that it was a scientific research center, and, for some reason, the subject of research had to be kept secret. Of course, that same secret had turned into a global nightmare in the past few days!

"System restored," an artificial female voice stated. "System requires re-specification of personnel. The system is unable to identify. Personnel identification records have been lost!"

The soldiers looked at each other for a few seconds.

One of the soldiers shrugged as if to say, "What do we do now?"

"We wait," the leader answered. "They'll try to bypass those requests via satellite from Washington and then we'll take action."

Indeed, no more than five minutes had passed before the female voice again came from the speakers.

"Please wait...system initiation...

"Welcome Mr. W, F, T, A, S, J, T, U, O, R, B and C. Status report: Incubators inactive. Embryos have expired. Farm cages, report:

Cage C1/ EMPTY

Cage C2/ EMPTY

Cage C3/ EMPTY

Cage C4/ EMPTY

Cage C5/ EMPTY

Cage C6/ EMPTY

Cage C7/ EMPTY

Cage C8/ EMPTY

Cage C9/ DEAD ANIMAL

Cage C10/ EMPTY

Cage C11/ DEAD ANIMAL

Cage C12/ EMPTY

Cage C13/ DEAD ANIMAL

Cage C14/ EMPTY

Report on compartments for guests: unable to access, possible short circuit, examination is ordered. Analysis showed: worrying percentages of D22 by product, result: possible escape of hatchling, examination should be conducted. Percentages of methane in the atmosphere: unable to calculate, examination is ordered. Monitor 13, list of proportions of atmosphere's components, examination and verification.

"CAUTION. Limited energy supplies, remaining operation time approximately 13 minutes; I repeat, operation time 13 minutes!"

Now time wasn't simply against them, it was at war with them. Everything had to be done quickly. There wasn't enough time to send all the lists and records from this computer's hard disks to Washington. The mission was going to fail. Humanity would have one more reason to lose hope.

The commander didn't pause to think about it for long. He reached a decision in a fraction of a second and, taking the initiative, he found the switches on the electrical board that controlled the building's lighting and turned them off. At that instant, the light vanished and everything was plunged into darkness.

Everybody understood what their leader hoped to do. Maybe they could buy some time, even a few minutes, by minimizing the unnecessary waste of energy. They couldn't switch on their helmet lamps without risking attracting unknown organisms, and they didn't like the idea of operating in absolute darkness, but they were ready to face anything and at whatever cost.

The commander signaled that a special device that detected life forms by tracking respiration should be inserted through the hole on the mirror. Measurements showed that there was nothing there. One by one, the soldiers passed through the opening and secured the large room they entered.

The place was some sort of control room, filled with computers both operative and inoperative. The number of desks in there suggested that the whole operation wasn't just secret but gigantic as well, with plenty of staff. The undertaking must have required a base equipped with every kind of scientist and technician. Of course, now the only residents were mice and flies, and maybe something else too…

One of the soldiers removed his gas mask to smell the air, and nearly suffocated. The whole place stank, and the air was so stale that survival without the masks would be impossible. The amount of methane in the air exceeded tolerable limits.

Another soldier moved quickly towards the other end of the vast room while the rest stayed behind, covering him. He didn't get to the other end of the room, but simply stopped midway and stood there, frozen in place.

The leader, unaware of what had made the soldier freeze, ordered two others to follow him from either side to ascertain what was going on. They had almost drawn even with him when he heard them and raised his hand in a signal for them to stop. Then he activated his radio.

"We've got company!" he said.

"We have no indications on the device," its operator replied. "If you're sure, then proceed cautiously; we've nine people back here to cover you."

"Negative, the enemy is not in front of us."

"What do you mean?"

"If I'm not mistaken, I have an animal in front of me, I believe it's a panther, with its intestines spilled all over the floor!"

"And what's that got to do with us?"

"Sir, this is very important. The dead animal's body is still steaming!"

"Message received, stay alert. Keep going," the leader said calmly.

One of the three soldiers on point moved slowly to the other end of the room.

"The room has been secured," the leader said. "William, you take it from here."

A soldier specially skilled in computers approached one of the desks. The desk held two monitors, both on, along with a keyboard and a mouse. The soldier pulled a paper out of his pocket and leaned over the desk, grasping the timeworn mouse. The operating system wasn't familiar, although it reminded him of the common windowed environment. It had most likely been developed to support the needs of a highly specialized and safe network. The only thing sure, however, was that if William couldn't operate this system, things would be very, very difficult.

Two more soldiers joined him. Struggling against time, he was trying to connect the local network with the satellite, constantly moving the mouse and keyboarding with unbelievable speed, oblivious to all else around him. Now, everything was up to him, and he knew that very well!

Sweat covered his face but he didn't have time to wipe it-he didn't have time for anything unnecessary.

"Seven minutes until shut down," the computer announced. Something inside each of them, something none of them ever wanted to believe, told them that they would never have the chance to learn if those few minutes would be enough to save millions of lives...

Their device sounded, detecting something. Three organisms had entered the building and, at that moment, they were coming down the ladder. There were only a few seconds left!

"I'm done!" William said, relieved, without realizing what was going on. The others immediately signed for him to be quiet, but it was too late. The dinosaurs had sensed their presence and were approaching.

The soldiers took position as quickly and noiselessly as possible; some in corners, others behind desks, all looking at one point, the spot were they expected the predators to appear. Their gun-sights were also pointing at that spot-humanity's weapons turned upon its own weapons! Who could predict the outcome of such a battle?

They waited, ready to die, aware that they would die, but ready to give a fight and lose it the way only they knew how. And if the moment didn't come, when the animals' eyes came into view like yellow full moons seen through a chink in a wooden jail, then they could hold their heads high and say, "I didn't hesitate for a moment!"

But the trigger is something that can be pressed so easily, and the bullet is something that travels so fast, to end up painting those full moons red. That's how the first animal went down, without realizing what had hit it. It died in ignorance, but the sound of the shot and the creature's death in the only entrance to the room warned the two animals behind it. More gunshots shattered the gigantic mirror, but didn't penetrate to hit the animals behind it. The two live creatures fled far away."Uploading will take approximately two and a half minutes; I believe the remaining energy is enough," William reported.

"I want you to confirm the completion of the data transfer."

"Be sure about that, although, if the transfer isn't completed in the first try, I don't believe there'll be time left to overcome the problem."

"Okay," the leader said, then ordered two of the men guarding the entrance to follow him. All three of them headed towards the end of the room.

A big metal door blocked their way. On the wall next to it a keyboard lit up with symbols and numbers. The leader approached it and pressed nine zeros in a row.

"Dangerous amounts of toxic gases, possible leak. The room will be evacuated," the computer voice said. The two soldiers looked at each other.

"Command to all team members. Activate protection against biological weapons. The gases that will come out of this door will not be pleasant."

"Access approved," the computer voice said, and the large door began opening.

A cloud of white gas spread over the ground, covering the soldiers' boots. No one knew what affect the gas would have on skin or, even worse, upon the men's lungs, and nobody wanted to imagine. The gases had damaged the walls that had contained them.

"I want a sample of air from the upper and lower levels. Take it quickly before our movements agitate the layers that formed during the time this place remained isolated from the world outside."

"The samples are ready."

"How much time do we have left until the system's collapse?"

"One minute and thirty five seconds."

"Is transfer complete?"

"Count eight seconds and I'm done."

"Very well; Dennis, David, get to the end of the corridor. We're looking for a door labeled Defensive Biological Engineering, or the initials DBE."

The two young men walked down the hallway, each checking his side for the room where the biological weapons that would exterminate the predators had been developed. An entire government was counting on the records and studies they would find in that room.

"I've found the door," one of the two soldiers said.

"Open it by keyboarding nine zeros; if that doesn't work, shoot it down!" the leader ordered.

"Power failure in forty-five seconds!" someone announced.

"It seems that this is as far as the electricity goes."

"Transfer is complete; there won't be any problem if the electrical supply ends, will there?" the soldier next to the leader asked.

The commander looked at him, although the big mask he had on hid his eyes. "Guys, I believe there's something you should know. The reason we're alive and have avoided the predators' attack up till now is because the station's defensive system was activated along with the rest of the system."

"I don't understand, what system are you talking about?"

"Did you wonder why the animals ran off?"

"Because we shot at them."

"Unfortunately, we didn't drive them away, the station's security system did. The station automatically limits the vision of the animals by preventing the pupil of their eyes to dilate relative to the present light. When the animals came to find us, they were, without exaggeration, nearly blind! "

"Five seconds!"

"Caution, the system will terminate function. Replace energy sources and restart when possible," the computer said just before the computer monitors and several scattered indicator lights went dark. The soldiers' night vision glasses allowed them to see green-tinged images.

"Did you open the door?" the commander asked the two soldiers at the DBE door.

"The door is open, sir."

"Good; well, what are you waiting for? Get inside, while we still have time, before the predators return."

"We're already inside sir, the area has been secured," one of them said.

"Put any document you find in there in the special bags you were given. Hurry up!"

"Yes sir," both soldiers acknowledged. They had already opened the special, reinforced bags they had with them, and rapidly filled two bags with the contents of the desk drawers and the wall shelves. Most of the papers they had gathered seemed useless, worn by time and the adverse conditions. But the soldiers knew they weren't qualified to make decisions.

"We're done, we have two almost-full bags," one soldier reported.

"Seal the bags and come-" The leader didn't complete his sentence. Something had stopped him from talking-the reappearance of the predators.

They wished the detection device was broken, they wished they were anywhere else but there, but none of those wishes came true. It was unknown whether the sixteen organisms were velociraptors or not, but they were coming unhurriedly down the big ladder. They outnumbered the people, and as dangerous as an entire army. They were death embodied, coming down the stairs of Hades one by one, to welcome the newcomers to the realm of death.

"Everybody take your position!" the leader whispered over the radio. "When the fight ends, I want each of you to tell me how many he killed!"

"Yeah, right," one of the soldiers said, and crossed himself.

"Fire!" was the last command heard before screams and roars dominated the polluted air. The predators didn't withdraw, they had no reason to do so.

"Don't stop, they're in!"

"Fuck, they're too many, too many!"

They kept shooting. Bodies, some human, some predator, dropped to the floor and convulsed until their last breaths. The darkness hid scenes of unimaginable horror, mind-numbing scenes. But eventually, even those who avoided the strikes of the predators and didn't get anything more than a simple scratch or a cut on their uniform, succumbed to the poisonous gases.

"Help...help me," a disoriented soldier mumbled as he crawled on the floor. No one had time to deal with the last minutes of a dying man. There was a war going on in there. Men dropped dead under talons that cut through their bodies, without even realizing where they had come from. Bullets killed the predators.

It was merely a matter of time and numbers. Which side would leave the last member standing; what species would the last survivor belong to? Darkness covered the terrifying truth, and the silence that spread a while later covered even more. Nothing moved, there was no gunshot, no twitter, just a radio, saying, "This is Washington, progress report...I repeat..."

Those in Washington waited for an answer, but the answer wasn't given in human speech. Something had indeed survived in there, something that didn't speak any human language but just twittered...

Nobody in Washington knew that language, but they all knew what the sound of it meant, and they all cried for the twelve men who had died...

BACK TO WASHINGTON

"There have been no signs of life for over three minutes now, Mr. President. We'll probably have to consider them dead."

"I knew that's how it would end up," Clive said.

"But don't forget what this whole operation brought in return, even if the people who took part in it never come back. Those kids didn't die for nothing!"

"Definitely not. Inform their families, tell them that their children, by their death, might have saved the world; make them feel proud."

"Mr. President," the Defense Secretary said, "the information collected by the satellite is ready for processing."

"Go on," Clive said, well aware of what the disclosure of the 'farm's' data would mean for him and several others.

"Yes sir. Forty-five scientists in total, all over the world, will be simultaneously processing the data we provide. I hope we haven't done all this for nothing."

"I hope that too, not only because I wouldn't like the lives of those kids to be lost for nothing," Clive said, and added to himself, "as well as mine." "But also because I believe this data we have in our hands is our only hope."

BELIEVE

"Mr. President, I'm sorry to bother you, but there's some archaeologist raising the roof; I think Robert Gallon is his name."

"What does he want from me?"

"To warn you, he said; that's what I heard him saying!"

"To warn me about what?"

"Well, look; I told him that you don't have time. If you want we can throw him out right now-we would have already done so, but there are the TV reporters out there and, well, you understand…"

"Let him in; I have time until the results of the analysis are received. Let him in."

"Yes sir," the officer said and left, almost running to tell the bodyguards to release Gallon and let him enter the room where President Clive waited.

"At last, Mr. President! I know your time is valuable but you have to listen to me," Gallon said breathlessly.

"You're right about my time; say what you have to say quickly. I actually heard you want to warn me!"

"That's right, Mr. President."

"About what?"

"It has to do with Manhattan; if you don't listen to me, you'll very soon come to a dead end!"

"What could you possibly know about Manhattan that I don't?"

"Many things, Mr. President; believe me, many things!"

"Such as?"

"Such as the velociraptors' capabilities. I forgot to tell you, I've studied archaeology and biology; I work in this field, and I've also written a paper for MIT; I could show it to you if you like," he said, and was about to open his bag when two men grabbed his hands, preventing him from finishing his action.

"Why in God's name would I be interested in your paper?" Clive asked.

"Oh, but it's about the velociraptors' swimming ability; I worked over a year to complete it!"

"Mister...?"

"Gallon, that's my name."

"Mr. Gallon, we have scientists all over the world who work with us via the Web. Let them decide how to handle this, they know better."

"But, how could they know better? They didn't work more than a day before reaching a conclusion. Mr. President, I know they asserted that velociraptors cannot swim, but it's not true."

"I don't have anymore time, please trust your colleagues and leave."

"But, in the name of God, at least order an evacuation of all the people near New York, and don't just tell them they're safe!"

"Sir, this meeting is finished," Clive said, and drew away. The two bodyguards grabbed the scientist by his arms and started leading him out.

"At least take a look at these!" Gallon shouted, and he dropped the bag he carried. "It won't take you more than a minute, but you could save thousands of people!"

The door closed and the desperate man's shouts were lost behind it.

"What shall I do with it?" a bodyguard asked, holding up Gallon's bag.

Clive turned and looked at the Secretary of Defense as if requesting help in his decision.

The Secretary winced, and told him to throw it away.

"There can't be so many mistaken people, get rid of it!" Clive said with a heavy heart. And he indeed acted correctly, according to the mindset of so many great people of our times. He made calculated the odds at twenty to one against Gallon's theory, but he had forgotten to multiply by the proper factor!

OUT OF CONTROL!

So far, two cities at the extremes of the earth were utterly destroyed, millions of people were dead, and thousands of predators roamed free in North America and Australia. Some predators had been reported in Asia. Only New York city had limited their spread to only one of its municipalities: Manhattan.

No one believed that everything was under control; even the politicians, who normally presented the rose-colored perspective for everything bad, were now silent., They were looking truth right in the eyes.

And what was that truth? Maybe that mankind was weak, unable to control the power it had grasped, or maybe the fact that the strongest survive in this world while the weaker vanish. If the moment eventually came when the last person struck by a predator dropped to their knees, what would it be that knocked them down-mankind's weakness or his power? Because although humanity thinks it isn't simply powerful but all-powerful, it lacks the strength, the courage to admit we aren't the most powerful.

Throughout history, humanity created gods and believed in them, invented entities considered superior to people, and became slave to its own imagination. The only thing that could kill man was man himself. But sometimes, mankind makes its creations better than itself. In this case, the creation was much better!

MANHATTAN

A dead city is definitely a hard thing to view. The lights aren't turned on at night, the avenues are empty of cars, the schools hold no children, and velociraptors, not pedestrians, come and go almost undisturbed, seeking fresh meat to carry back to dens located underground or in some dark building.

The monsters had multiplied in number; the scientists estimated the population would soon reach a thousand. This time the margin of error disregarded in the first debacle at Sydney had been accounted for. Of course, knowing how numerous your enemy is doesn't necessarily make you the winner, but it's an advantage. At least, for as long as the predators remained isolated on Manhattan Island.

The whole world watched the situation in Manhattan through their television sets, which kept the public constantly informed. Some people didn't watch from afar, however, but actively participated in the isolation of Manhattan. They had literally surrounded the borough. War machines were set up on the opposite shore, in New Jersey, the Bronx and Long Island to prevent the predators from escaping-an unimaginable possibility! Vigilance slackened with the lapse of days. The predators didn't seem to like the damp weather. Personnel were moved to reinforce other areas.

Not more than two thousand remained to surround that borough of New York. The inactivity and the constant waiting with nothing happening was somehow reassuring. They grew careless, and they underestimated their opponents.

"How many hours have you been awake?" Dominic, one of those two thousand soldiers, asked.

"Don't ask" Ivan said, looking at him. "Besides, you know as well as I."

"I believe that after a whole sixteen hours, they should have replaced us," Dominic complained. "Who gives a shit about us? They only look after themselves."

"It's not that I disagree, but look, we're in an emergency situation," Ivan said. "It's acceptable to-"

"You're telling me it's acceptable? Do you know what's on the other side? Of course you know, but I'll remind you. There are some very strange little animals over there, and if they see you in front of them, you'll stop seeing. The last thing you'll touch before you breathe your last will be your little stomach-if you're lucky, of course, because otherwise-"

"Shut up!" Ivan protested, "you've just made me forget I'm hungry!"

"You didn't like it?"

"When you don't have some things, it's nice to dream of them. Why do I sit here with you? You're an animal!"

"They're animals too, pal, and you know something?" Dominic said.

"What?"

"It seems to me like these animals are going to win, just like they always do!"

"Now you're making me mad."

"That's my specialty!" Dominic quipped.

"You think I don't know? We've studied and worked together-"

"Hey, why are you talking in the past tense?"

"I don't know," Ivan replied. "I really don't know how it came to me!"

"Anyway, in case this, this past tense will become a reality, I want you to know that…"

"You want me to know what, my friend?"

Dominic was suddenly embarrassed. "What you just said!"

"And that is?" Ivan pressed.

"That we were, are and-I hope-will always be friends."

"For a lifetime!" Ivan said, and held out his hand.

"Yes, old friend, for a life-"

Dominic never finished the word; he never spoke again. His mouth remained open, as if it couldn't bring itself to say the word, but instead of words, blood tumbled out. Instead of sound, tears ran down his cheeks. And then-then he died.

He was the first victim of the animals swimming to the shore opposite Manhattan, but he wasn't the only one. That day, two thousand died; no one survived. And all that because of a human mistake, an unconsidered estimation.

The man who had made the mistake didn't pay with his life that day. Humanity, however, definitely paid for his mistakes, and the punishment inflicted was the one deserved. Accountability and debts wouldn't end there; they would continue. History wrote about such a period; an unknown poet said that, at the end of the account, our end would come. That prediction came true much sooner for some than for others; for others, it was sufficient that history was still being written…

Some others-brave ones-weren't satisfied with that…

DEAD END!

"Fire them all!" the president shouted, rousing everybody in his office. "How can it be possible-the jerks! They call themselves scientists, and I believed them...destroy them!"

"Mr. President, calm down," his friend Vincent Winslow said. That man must have had a lot of courage; no one else wanted to stand next to the furious president; everybody liked it when he was an openhanded, calm president.

"What are you saying, tell me," Clive sputtered, "do you know what you're telling me?"

"I'm telling you to calm down sir; we need you."

"Need what? What kind of lies are you telling now? Do you know, my friend, what I did a while ago? Tell me."

"It wasn't your mistake!" Winslow protested.

"Go and tell that to the press, the television stations, the families and relatives of those who will die after the predators' escape," Clive said. For a moment, it seemed to those around him that the president's eyes grew moist, but they weren't sure.

Winslow didn't come up with an answer this time. There wasn't one.

"I can't believe it, they've escaped and now they're at large in America. Damn me, I nearly believed we had everything under control, but after this-"

"Mr. President, there's still hope," the Secretary of Defense said.

"What are you saying? That the dinosaurs will suddenly say, 'sorry to bother you' and leave? You know very well that something like that will never happen!"

"Mr. President, you have to speak seriously, if you want an answer."

"No problem!" Clive said and stood up in front of him. "Answer me seriously, what can we do?"

"You won't like the answer, but it's the only solution," the Secretary warned.

Clive looked at him strangely. "What do you mean?" he asked.

"I'll say it in two words: nuclear attack!"

The president's look changed to one of horror; he remained silent for a while. "For the first time in my career, as God is my witness, I want to object, but I can't!"

"Maybe because…maybe because it's our only solution, sir."

"No! God damn me, no! This can't be out only solution," Clive retorted.

"You said it yourself; we're at a dead end," Winslow said.

"Yes, but a nuclear attack? It would destroy everything and us, together"

"But not all of us," the Secretary reminded him. "Most of us would survive."

"I don't know," Clive said. "The decision is very serious and we have to make it right away, before the animals spread across America. Call for the Congressional committee to meet immediately."

"Yes, Mr. President," the Secretary said.

"It seems we have to make a very serious decision, a final decision," Clive said thoughtfully, gazing absently at the opposite wall as if seeing right through it. At that moment, everybody wished he could actually do so.

HOPE

Daniel and Nancy and Clara escaped from the building they had entered to avoid the velociraptors. They didn't know whether to run or hide. Hunger and exhaustion showed on their faces; they looked ready to collapse.

"Mum, I can't go on anymore," Nancy said as her mother dragged her away from the spot where they had killed the deinonychus.

"I know it, sweetie," Clara said, "but you have to, it can't be otherwise."

"But it's no use wandering around."

"We're not just wandering, we're trying to get to the shore, the port, or somewhere where they can see us."

"See us," Daniel whispered. That sentence caused ripples, as though a pebble had dropped into the lake of his mind. Somewhere there, an idea surfaced-an idea of how they could survive!

"What's up, Daniel?" Clara asked.

"Well, I had a thought. It's not necessary to get to the coast for them to see us. There are other places, as well!"

"Like where?"

"Come on! I wonder why we didn't think of it earlier. Our troubles could have been over long ago."

Nancy and Clara stared at him with expressions of curiosity and bewilderment.

"I mean the roofs of the buildings!" Daniel exclaimed. "If we started a fire on a tall building, perhaps they would see us and come at our rescue."

"Daniel is right," Nancy said enthusiastically, looking at her mother. "There are a lot of helicopters flying up there; one of them will see us!"

Clara turned her eyes to the sky. Could their savior possibly come from up there? She hoped yes, not because she was worried about herself-that didn't even cross her mind-but because she wanted to rescue the two innocent children with her, especially her daughter.

"It won't be so easy but it's worth a try," Clara said in support of Daniel's idea. "Follow me; I know exactly which building we must go to." She led the way, pulling the exhausted little girl by the hand again.

FACING THE DANGER OF EXTINCTION!

THE SECOND COUNCIL

They had gathered, all those gentlemen who govern the course of our lives, in a spacious, round room. A round table occupied most of the space in the middle of the room, proclaiming its importance with its great size. Maybe it was hoped that its costly wood and solid chairs made those sitting around it think better, but that was doubtful.

Fortunately, or perhaps unfortunately, many prominent people sat around that table that day. They were there to discuss and reach a decision, good or bad. They wouldn't be deciding only for themselves but, in a strange way, for all of humanity, and mistakes now could not be corrected later. The responsibility was enormous and they had realized that, maybe for the first time in their lives.

They all sat around the large wooden monster talking to each other and creating a kind of formal fuss. The conversations stopped very quickly when another, more official person arrived. The president quickly entered the room and sat in his chair. This time no one stood at his appearance, to honor him. This time, they all felt the breath of death drawing closer than at any other time. This time, they were more selective, more conscious of consequences.

"All of you know what a terrible tragedy the blockade of Manhattan turned into," Clive said, studying the faces of the council members for signs of agreement. Indeed, they all nodded. "We're here to find a way to prevent the further spread of the animals. I have a solution to suggest, along with the Secretary of Defense, but I'd first like to hear your suggestions. So, does anyone have any feasible, realistic solutions to put forward?"

Only two people raised their hands, something admittedly unusual, but in this case, it was rather more than enough.

"You can speak," the president said, pointing at one of the two presumptive saviors of humanity.

"Thank you," the congresswoman said. "The solution I have to suggest will probably not satisfy our needs immediately, but I believe that if we waited for a while, it would bring a lot in return."

"We haven't got time to waste, but go on!"

"But it wouldn't be a waste of time to wait for the results of...of the tests. You know..." She trailed off as Clive frowned. "I believe what the tests will reveal will be very important; I mean, in terms of facing the problem, that is."

"Of course," the president said, but he scowled at the woman belligerently.

"At this point, I don't think it's bad to say it. Besides, the country is in a crisis, but the threat of a government collapse is unlikely."

"To say what?" someone blurted.

"Mr. President?" the woman prompted.

"I want you to know that I don't feel like I'm pleading," Clive said. "Illegal activity took place and I was an accomplice in that-," several shifted in their chairs, as if sensing the foundations of authority relent "-activity that, with my help, had to do with the present situation."

Everyone was trying to look him in the eyes, as if pitying him, as if watching a dying man they couldn't help. He couldn't meet their eyes. None of them spoke, they let him finish.

"The design and creation of these creatures was work I financed and concealed; I and others in this room and from the outside. We collaborated with one company in particular, one called NeoGene.

The operation, whose goal was to upgrade our future military force with living biological weapons, was abandoned two years ago, due to some unpredictable events. All the turmoil now occurring is the result of my mistakes!"

The members of Congress remained still in their seats, as if they had heard the most horrible fable in the world. That's almost what the president's words sounded like to the unsuspecting ears of most of them; like a great lie, like the nightmare that would tear down their careers, if their lives weren't terminated first. It was now a matter of time before the government was broken by factions placing blame and denying responsibility.

The Secretary of Defense now revealed his own guilt. "I was also aware of the farm-I mean, the program," he said, looking at the floor, unable to face the others' eyes.

It wasn't long before the first reactions occurred.

"Do you know what you're telling us? Have you considered even for a moment what your words mean? How in the name of God can you call what is happening merely a turmoil?"

"I don't think that we have time to argue at such a mom-"

"Of course not! At least, that's what's in your best interest now, just as it was then!"

"It's not in my interest; it's in the interest of mankind, God damn it!" Clive protested. "Look around you and see what's happening. I confessed and I'm ready to be punished, but you don't understand that, if it happens now, there will be so much time lost that this situation will be irreversible!"

"And what do you propose?" somebody demanded.

"Don't talk to anyone, at least for the time being. After things are under control, then do whatever you like!"

"But how can something like this be kept a secret?"

"It can, if you want it to!" Clive said in a loud voice. "I don't think there's anyone in here who wants to see humanity annihilated, is there?"

"You've handled it very well, Mr. President; congratulations," one congressman said, "but unfortunately, I cannot collaborate with assassins. I quit right now!"

"For Christ's sake, you can't draw back now!" Clive replied. "Nothing has changed for you, for any of you! My life is ruined, either way. But you have no right to abandon the people at such a time; they need us now!"

"Honestly Mr. President, are these the same thoughts you had when you approved the creation of such murderous organisms? I don't think so."

"I've regretted it a thousand times since then, but at least I can accept responsibility and I don't pull away."

The members of Congress looked at each other. They exchanged looks and whispers, and eventually seemed to agree with one another.

"Just for the time being," one of them said. "But be sure, you won't avoid the poison of the injection, neither you, nor anybody else who's involved in this. We owe it to all those who have lost their lives!"

Clive looked at the man. His face was stiff, devoid of emotion, as if the blood had stopped in his veins. "I have no objection," he said and wished that he would never regret his words. Now he wouldn't fight to save his life, which was doomed, but the lives of others.

"Is there any objection to keeping the President's involvement secret?" asked the same man who had pronounced the death sentence on the most powerful man on earth. No one objected. "So, what is the next issue? Another surprise, maybe?"

"Someone else had an idea on how to deal with the spread of the creatures," Clive said.

"I, I was the one."

"What do you have in mind?" Clive asked the man.

"The same thing as before, sir. I also believe that, now more then ever, we must wait for the results. Besides, they're human creations, there must be some contingency plan provided by their designers for such cases. Perhaps you might know...?"

"At this moment I know nothing more than you do," Clive said. "They didn't keep me up-to-date on everything they did, you know. The three members of the administrative council of NeoGene could give us a lot of information, if they were still alive of course…"

"What happened to them?"

"Two of them died from a strange virus, which was covered up; the other one was down there, in the Amazon, when the accident happened."

"So, the only thing we can do is wait."

"No, not exactly!" the president said. "There's one potential solution!"

"And what is that?" one of the members asked. Clive indicated the Secretary of Defense.

"I will say it in a nutshell, gentlemen," the Secretary said. "Nuclear attack!"

Everyone around him fell silent, although the bomb hadn't gone off yet.

There was a moment when everyone tried to speak at once, probably to object to the suggestion that had been made. The meeting was disrupted by shouting people.

Clive attempted to restore order. "Stop it all, of you! Shut up!" he shouted, and managed to silence everyone. "Whether you like it or not, however painful it might sound, there is no other solution!"

"So, you call the nuclear attack a solution? I'm sorry, but I call it suicide!"

"And what do you consider a solution? Sitting around and waiting, perhaps?"

"Definitely not!"

"Then what?" Clive asked. When no one answered, he went on. "Time is still on our side; we can still destroy them because they haven't managed to spread everywhere. Some areas will be irreversibly stricken, thousands of people will die by our own hands, but-"

"But we will survive, right?" somebody called sarcastically from the back of the room.

"Humanity will survive and, with it, dreams for a better world!"

"People like you will have no place in such a world, Clive, so please don't use such arguments."

Clive ignored the remark. "There is also something else you should consider, something self-evident, but I'll clarify it for you."

The members of the council looked at him as though they couldn't hear anything worse than they already had.

"If you agree to the use of nuclear technology, you must take into consideration that the first place to be bombed will be New York!"

Again they shifted in their seats. Some held their heads, some looked away, aching for the victims of their own attack, because the attack would be on their own homes, their own people.

"I know it sounds terrible," Clive said. "But no other country will permit us using nuclear weapons on its soil unless we do the same thing first on our own soil!"

"What if…" The speaker's voice trailed off.

"Say what you thought; we are in need of good ideas"

"I don't know if it's a good idea. It might sound stupid but, think of it: at this moment, the whole world is experiencing a great nightmare. We could take the chance and take action without permission or agreements!"

"What are you saying?" Clive asked.

Those who realized what was being discussed shuddered.

"I mean exactly what you think, Mr. President. Some day in the future, they'll be grateful to us."

"There's no place in the world where the people are ever going to say 'thank you for leaving half of us alive,' even if that's the only way for them to survive! If something like that happen, you have to know that no one is going to approve of our decisions. We'll probably be buried along with those we struck down with our weapons, with one difference-they will have been praised!"

Silence occupied the room for a while. Then the president. "However, it's an opinion, and since this is a democracy, I'm obligated to ask how many of you agree. We'll vote."

The members of the council looked at each other, considering their country first and then everything else. They thought of their loved ones first, and forgot those in other countries. They considered and decided first for homeland, for love, for life…regardless of the fact that they themselves had written in their books that, in earth's history, the most valuable thing on earth was a microscopic cell that lived before us all. Love and homeland came later..

Man runs so fast on the road of progress that it was merely a matter of time before he would stumble and lose control. The bad thing is that, at the speed of an Einstein-like mind, a simple pebble is enough to take you off course. To return to the course however, you unfortunately need a crane.

Some of them felt shame, others felt nothing. It was so logical, after all. They raised their hands, agreed to devastate the houses of those who hadn't voted for them, and managed to believe they were helping the world.

Clive, a man who had already lost his life and knew how valuable it was, and could see his brother in the eyes of a stranger, stepped back. His eyes were like those of a father catching his son shooting up on heroin. He was already enough of an assassin to be able to become even more, but he was the only one who didn't raise his hand in that room.

"Apparently you agree to the nuclear attack!" he said in a voice heavy with disappointment. "Let it be so. But know only this: Christ won by dying. He chose to kill himself first, and he never died. You have chosen to kill the others first."

No one answered; no one showed remorse."But I have something to say before this meeting is adjourned," Clive said in an imposing voice. "I state that I don't support the nuclear attack anymore. I vote against it!"

Murmurs of dissent rose in the room. Some members even stood, protesting the unexpected change in attitude from the most official member of their government.

"You can't change your mind now! Don't try to get out of it."

"What the hell has made you change your opinion?"

Similar questions came from many different mouths.

Clive tried to make himself heard. "In the beginning...I'm saying that, in the beginning, I wasn't sure of what I was going to do. It was because of your reaction, your decision; but not only because of that! I considered the innocent children that the velociraptors have gathered over their dens, oh, damn them! We couldn't blow up the buildings then because we faced the eyes of those children. It would be immoral to kill them from afar, they're not to blame for anything. It will be a disaster, a suicide, it will be-"

"Our only solution, Clive. You said that, not us!"

"I don't know, I don't..."

"But I do, Mr. President," someone else said. "You're too cowardly, too irresponsible to make such a decision!"

"It could be that, too," Clive admitted and lowered his head. "You can say I agree, I will not try to obstruct anyone in the completion of the mission. Be sure about that."

They all looked terrified, as if they'd met the man speaking in front of them for the first time.

"You should know," he said, "that I wish we will all die before we see the deformed smile of a child from one of the villages we bomb."

"But that's the smile we're going to kill for, Clive."

Clive turned to him. "I want you to listen to your words, young man," he told the speaker. "I want you to tell me how can a word like 'smile' can be in the same sentence with the word 'kill'!" The speaker didn't answer, and Clive resumed. "Maybe that's why we've reached this point. You would tell me, of course, and justifiably, that I've confused fiction with reality; in this world, evil is only fought with evil! But I also have something to tell you, even if it makes no difference anymore. It's not my mistake; it's the mistake of somebody else who lived long before us, when the word 'human' was only beginning to take on its meaning! That man first confused fiction with reality. You see, thinking brought reason and that brought a million harms. Some prefer it this way, and they're not wrong-no one is wrong in this case, and that's the tragic part. We're used to the judge trying the defendant, but never before have defendant and judge been the same person!"

He lowered his eyes and said in a low voice, "I don't know why I said all this, I guess this outburst was something I had to do." He turned his eyes to one of the paintings hanging on the wall. "I suppose we weren't ready," he whispered. "We weren't ready to face ourselves!"

He turned and left.

After a while, the room where great decisions were made was left empty, and the only face left in it was the faded, mute face in the painting. The first man who had managed to win was nailed on a cross, without ever having held a gun in his hands.

BARRY
*T*HE DEATH

The mental institution was quieter than ever before. At the beginning, a few screams had been heard, a few cries, and then, stillness. The attendants had left the inmates to God's mercy and run off when they heard that the predators had escaped from Sydney. No one would blame them; besides, they left the doors behind them open, for all the lunatics who were sane enough to wish to run away.

Barry was one of those sane lunatics, but he didn't try to escape the death that approached. Maybe because he knew better than everyone that, however fast he ran, however loud he screamed, it would all be futile.

He was standing up and looking out the window of his room. There were a few dead people, some pools of blood, and every now and then, some strange animals crossing the courtyard. The right creatures in the right place, one would say, and he wouldn't be wrong at all.

The sight didn't daunt Barry at all, however ominous the implications were for his life and the lives of the others. Besides, he had seen the same scene a thousand times in his sleep. This couldn't be any more difficult than coming to terms with the horror and learning to live with it until it was flesh and blood. Barry knew there wasn't a chance in a million that man would escape the bloodthirsty jaws of the predators. Not even one!

He had asked the attendant who had unlocked the doors of the little rooms and shouted, "Go away, run for your lives!" to leave his door locked. The attendant had hesitated at first, but Barry reminded him of the reason he was brought there; he reminded him that everything that was happening was as crazy as his allegations had been when he'd been brought there. As a sensible man, he had the right to decide his destiny. And that was what the attendant considered as he did Barry the favor of leaving him locked in his little room, the place where he had lived all those years and the place where he was going to die.

He'd chosen not to fight for his life. It was the decision of a man that no one on earth had believed, not even his relatives; a man who was condemned to live buried inside four white walls with only the company of a terrible secret that unfolded every night in his nightmares. Barry was a man who had stopped dreaming and therefore hoping. Death, at the moment when everything around him justified his claims, would seem like deliverance.

Two quick bangs came on the door. Barry didn't bother to turn around and look; he knew very well what it was and what it wanted. His heart beat a little faster, he didn't know why. He stared at one of the dead bodies that lay in the courtyard. Scenes from the past came into his mind, scenes from the death of his friend, on a rainy night in a park like so many other parks.

His eyes shut. The door collapsed. Pain for his friend covered the pain in his body. He didn't feel sorry to leave the world even for a moment. Something inside him was whispering, "You'll go to him, you'll be together again, together for ever..."

His last breath passed over his lips and they formed a smile which would remain forever; no matter how dead the face was, that smile would always look like the lips that formed it still breathed...

HOPE LIVES UP THERE...

They had climbed up over thirty floors without stopping at any one of them. The fugitives' fatigue and hunger were becoming more intense, however. The two children were on the verge of collapse and Clara found the effort of dragging her daughter behind her sapping her strength, minute by minute. Their legs burned; their stomachs protested with terrible, strong aches.

The stairs seemed endless. The air was stuffy and the silence didn't allow them to calm down even for a moment, however strange that sounded! Somewhere above, though, as they climbed the last steps to the thirty-fifth floor, a welcome aroma pervaded the atmosphere in the stairwell. It was the smell of cooked food. The two children paused for a moment, then Daniel started running toward the source of the smell.

"Daniel, wait!" Clara shouted in vain. At that point, the boy's mind couldn't recognize danger; he wasn't afraid of the unknown; he knew only that he hadn't eaten for more than two days.

Nancy signed eagerly to her mother to follow and, although as exhausted and hungry as Daniel, they searched for him. After a while they found him holding a couple of cheese pies in one hand and a soft drink in the other. His mouth was smeared with crumbs left in his haste to chew and swallow, and he didn't bother stopping to speak and invite them to enjoy his finding-a small restaurant, with a view of Central Park. They were the only ones invited!

"You could have run into a monster," Clara admonished him.

"Stop it and eat," Daniel interrupted, spraying chunks of food as he spoke.

Nancy ran to the self-service counter, snatched up everything she saw, and started devouring it greedily. Clara didn't stay out of the party for long. After a while, they searched and found bottled water. They didn't trust the tap water; it could have been polluted, or poisoned by those outside in an attempt to kill the animals. Little did they know that the animals also avoided food and water coming from the outside world.A quarter hour later, Nancy and Daniel's bellies were swollen.

"Clara, are you on a diet?" Daniel asked.

"Very funny," she said disapprovingly.

"Fine, don't take it too hard. Phew! Well do you know what I'd like to do now?"

"What, Daniel?" Nancy asked.

"I'd like to take a long-a very long-nap!" He stretched his arms out to show how great his desire was.

"You probably can't take one," Clara said. She stood and indicated that the children should do the same. They rose resentfully but without complaining. Time was too valuable to waste it on arguing. They had to move steadily toward their goal; that was the only way they could be saved!

It took a long time and the last of their strength to reach the top floor. As they climbed the last steps, the idea of going down again seemed impossible to them; going any further up was, of course, impossible.

"Next time we should take the elevator," Daniel said, but nobody laughed. All eyes were fixed on the top of the staircase, wishing to see it end, yearning to see the precious sky outside the door. And they did see it end, only there was no sign of the sky, not even any light.

The door didn't open when Nancy tried the handle. Nancy started crying. Daniel just stood still and Clara held her face in her hands, despairing.

The door in front of them seemed locked, but it wasn't! Clara grasped the handle and turned it sharply, and the door burst open, revealing the sky.

Tears drying on their smiling faces, their eyes shining with relief, the trio stepped out onto the roof. But when they looked out on the rest of the world beyond Manhattan, questions rose in their minds. Where was the army; where were the helicopters that should have been flying over Long Island, Brooklyn and New Jersey? Why did everything seem to be as dead as Manhattan?

The same horrified thought crossed all their minds. The velociraptors had escaped from Manhattan and had conquered the whole of New York, maybe even the whole world! At first they refused to believe it, but it began to seem more and more logical.

"Oh my god!" Daniel whispered.

"You see what we see Daniel, right?" Nancy asked, shivering.

"I don't think so...I don't believe it! I think I see something more!"

"I don't dare to guess," Clara said without taking her eyes from the scene of death that lay in the distance.

"The bridges...the bridges aren't there anymore! Do you know what that means?"

"What?" Clara asked and closed her eyes as if she already knew the answer.

"Two things," Daniel said. "First, they've probably abandoned us." Nancy bit her lip. "And second, that the velociraptors can swim." They managed to escape across the water and killed an entire city! Now, I don't think there's anything that can stop them. Nothing!" he finished in a whisper.

"You're saying...you're saying we're going to die Daniel?" Nancy stared into his eyes.

"You should wish we're the only ones!" Daniel answered. At that moment, he realized there was no point in lying, no point at all.

FINALIZING THE DECISION!

There was nothing still in the War Room. The decision to use a hydrogen bomb had turned everything upside down, while the fact that the target countries wouldn't be notified of the attack loaded the atmosphere with even more tension. The whole idea sounded crazy, but it had a sound basis: the U.S was going to present their action as a demonstration of sympathy and assistance towards the disaster areas.

Clive paced up and down, taking care of the final details of the ambitious plan. Sweat ran down his face. His eyes were red with strain and fatigue. What they were attempting to do wasn't at all simple. They were aware that there was no chance of avoiding the accusations and rejection from the rest of the world, even if they did eventually manage to save planet Earth!

A young man ran into the big room, shouting the president's name. Clive raised his head and looked at the officer. His face showed fear, as if he had been dreading this moment.

"Mr. President," the officer panted out, "I have bad news!"

"How bad?" Clive asked, staring him in the eyes, hoping it wasn't what he expected.

"It depends on what you think of as bad. I was told to tell you that the possibility that it will withstand attack is more than 90%!"

"What will withstand, god damn it!"

The young man took a deep breath and then continued. "Well, the predators that have invaded the three cities are probably not just velociraptors."

"There is another species, too?"

"My information concerns New York. The watchers that check the situation from time to time from helicopters told me to inform you that we're probably dealing with a new species. Its name is deinonychus."

Clive closed his eyes. He had heard what he was most afraid of hearing.

"You never told us that!" a congressman whispered as passed by the president. Fortunately, the officer didn't hear the man's comment.

"I have a detailed report on the potential abilities of the new species," the young man said and placed a file on the desk next to him.

"Okay," the president said in a low voice, as if his voice had been deprived of all power. "Thank you; you can go now."

The officer hesitated. Clive searched his face. The man stood like a porter waiting for a tip rather than a government aide.

"What else do you have to tell me?" Clive asked.

"I expected you to ask questions," the young man answered, surprising Clive.

"What do you mean?" Clive asked.

"Well, you didn't even seem interested in learning whether deinonychus is more dangerous than the velociraptor!"

The president frowned. His tired mind had brought him to a difficult situation. "Well, we know a little bit about dinosaurs, as well," he said, and laughed to waylay any suspicion that could lead to the collapse of the government at such a crucial point.

"I see," the young man said, and laughed along with him. He left without asking any more questions.

Clive, however, felt the sweat on his face go cold at the thought that even deinonychus had survived the destruction of the farm. Although he had never opened a book on paleontology, he knew firsthand the deadly abilities of this new species. He remembered the words of one of those participating in the operation, now dead. The scientist had called them remarkable animals. They had gone up against velociraptors four to one, and won! Four velociraptors had been defeated by only one deinonychus!

He didn't want to think anymore. He had to notify the others of this tragic development, although something told him they had already found out. There wasn't any time for a second council. He ordered the announcement to be made over the speakers immediately.

"Where do we strike first, Clive?" one of the committee members asked. "After you left the meeting, most agreed to strike the area around Buenos Aires first."

"On what grounds?" Clive asked. Deep inside, he didn't care much about which of the two areas would be the first recipient of the destruction.

"We decided on Buenos Aires because the mission has a higher chance of success. We will also be able to control the massive opposition that will follow, at least at first. Opposition that could escalate into war."

"That sounds absolutely reasonable. Go on."

"Those are the main reasons. Of course, we counted on the fact that Australia is a continent, and therefore can be evacuated. The situation in Buenos Aires is more of a threat to the United States than Australia. Our reaction will seem more justified."

"That's all very correct," Clive said, then added, "now, I want you to tell me if you agree with the prohibition of a nuclear strike against New York."

The man standing opposite him jerked his head up, taking a deep breath. "What are you trying to do, Mr. President? Are you after a civil war, perhaps?"

"What I'm after is the most sensible thing one can think of. Consider what's going to happen if we let the velociraptors spread even further. In God's name, they'll reach Washington soon!"

"Wasn't it you who totally rejected a nuclear strike?"

"Of course it was me, and for your information, I still do. But don't you think that, if we are to sentence two of the infested areas to death, we should do the same with the third one, especially when that one belongs to us?"

"It sounds reasonable, Clive, but I don't think I know anyone who would condone showering radioactivity over the ground he walks on his entire life, on the ground where he was born and where he's going to die!"

"I can," the president said, but couldn't suppress a shudder. Neither of them spoke for a while.

"I knew you were ruthless, but I would have never imagined-"

"What I'm doing now doesn't require ruthlessness," Clive interrupted. "The only thing it requires is courage and sense at a moment when most people have lost both to panic."

"What you're saying, Clive, requires a man without feelings!" the man said, looking him in the eyes, giving Clive the impression that he felt sorry for him.

"I have no feelings, either. I stopped feeling after I made the mistake of approving a plan that ended up killing so many people." He blinked watery eyes. "After that, there's nothing worse I can do!"

The councilor lowered his head apologetically, but he said, "It was your choice, Clive. I can't do anything more than be silent and not betray our conversation. I cannot help."

"I understand," Clive said. "So, you and the others will let those animals spread beyond New York. In God's name, you know there's no turning back from there! Besides, if we bomb the other areas without doing the same to ourselves, we'll precipitate a world war!"

"Maybe. But no one will accuse me of treason. You said it yourself: one way or another, we're already dead. So, why not die in glory?"

"I can't believe that such a man dared to accuse me of the murder of so many millions of people!" Clive's tone turned from entreating to an aggressive, and the other man frowned. "At this moment, you're condemning a whole continent, and only God knows what's next."

"Fuck you," the councilor snapped, and turned and stalked away.

So the dialogue ended at a dead end. Men have never learned to surrender and so, men have never learned to lose one against the other.

Clive despaired. He watched an entire city gradually turning into a jungle and there was nothing he could do about it. He watched the thousands of velociraptors and the few dozen deinonychus believe me, they were enoughescaping from the city and spreading all over North America, reaching Los Angeles and taking over Washington.

Clive knew they would be viewers until the moment of regret came, the moment when they were all under the claws of dinosaurs. Only then would they realize what they had done, but it would be too late. Fortunately, that was all merely in Clive's head-for the time being. Something inside him told him that the moment of regret was getting closer and closer.

At some point he couldn't take the stress anymore. He collapsed on the floor. People ran to help him. Doctors entered the room almost immediately. But Clive was living his own dream, or perhaps, his own unique nightmare...he saw himself, and next to him, two little children were crying desperately. He saw a mother sitting in front of the children, trying to embrace them, but she had no arms! And then he saw a big mushroom cloud.

He stood up to face the wave racing towards him. The kids were still crying. The last teardrop never made it to the ground; it was lost, just as they were.

First the skin, then the flesh burned away, while they were still alive. And the mother couldn't do anything to protect them; she was melting like a lit candle that someone hadn't put out.

No, Clive wasn't lost in the force of the shock wave; rocks were condemned to survive that day and so did hearts made of stone!

The wave came and left, taking human souls and the souls of all living things with it. The dust settled and revealed the ruins of a city where the only living things were insects. Cockroaches crawled on what was left of the dead people's bodies.

Clive dreamt that many more people than they had estimated had survived in the cities before the blast. But along with their deaths had come the deaths of all the predators! Nothing had survived. That was the only fact to be thankful for.

But then, why had Clive's statuesque image sat on the ruined walls of a school to cry inconsolably, "Why?"

He awoke within seconds to see first a haze obscuring the faces of those standing above him. The haze quickly vanished.

"Are you all right?" a voice asked.

"Not at all," he answered, trying to get up.

"Would you like to take a sedative, anything...?"

"No, no, drugs can't help me."

"Whatever you think," the doctor said and the crowd that had gathered around him began scattering.

"We can't just stay inactive!" Clive shouted, so unexpectedly that everyone turned around to look at him. "We can't let the predators spread day by day, more and more. If the hydrogen bomb is our only solution, then let's use it, god damn it; let's use it on ourselves!"

They still stared at him but no one dared to say anything, not in front of so many people. That gave Clive the opportunity to assert himself.

"Don't you understand that it's totally immoral and inhumane to strike the other countries at this point?"

"One day they'll be grateful," someone broke in.

"That's wrong, very wrong. All of you are aware of the consequences of a nuclear attack. The hydrogen bomb may not have been tested in real-life conditions, but we all know what horrors it will unleash. All of us who are in this room, even the duty officers, will be condemned as war criminals, and our condemners won't be wrong-no, they'll be absolutely right!"

"You exaggerate."

"I might as well be exaggerating, and you know why? Because there won't be a human left alive to staff a court, to send us where we should go-that's how we're going to end up, because of our stupidity!"

A congressman advanced on Clive threateningly, holding Clive's eye with his glare. He stopped in front of him and whispered, "You said you weren't going to prevent it!"

Clive met his eyes and, without hesitation, answered in the same low voice, "I lied!"

"And what do you suggest?" Another councilor demanded, joining the conversation taking place in front of the terrified eyes of all the aides and clerks. None of them cared whether the conversation could later be leaked to the public by an ambitious listener.

"He's right Clive, what do you have to suggest?"

Clive thought about it for a while. Then he said, "Immediate attack with ground troops all over New York City!"

"What's the military strength you have in mind?"

Clive paused. "Seventy percent of the entire army, at least!"

Many objections arose and the room regained its noisy atmosphere. Only now, everybody talked about the same subject!

"That's beyond any reason, we'll have nothing left for later! There's no time to gather…"

"No, that's the only sensible thing to do, apart from using the hydrogen bomb, which I don't even want to consider. As far as time is concerned, most army units have already been called up to check the area around New York."

"All right, but have you considered what would follow if we lost?. It's our last hand and we shouldn't play all our cards at once."

"Time is working against us; soon it will be too late to play anything, can't you see that?"

"And what if they slaughter our troops? What if they set up a trap and everything ends in a few seconds?"

"But in God's name, we're talking about 70% of the armed forces!"

"We're talking about the worst enemy ever faced in the history of mankind!"

Clive had no response to that. "So, what do you think? Do you still believe that such an attack would be sensible?"

"As far as I'm concerned I think so!" someone sitting far from Clive said. "The greatest weapon of our enemy is neither its intelligence nor its speed. It's the creatures' rapid reproduction rate, the brief amount of time required for it to fill an entire city with its species!"

Surprised, Clive looked at the speaker. He hadn't expected anyone to support his opinion.

"He's right!" a voice called from the other side of the room. Now, questions and doubt showed on everybody's face, as they wondered if the ground troops should be allowed to start a war with their enemy. Within a minute, they were all convinced, although some would later regret their decision just moments before the attack, when the last hope of man would stand or vanish!

"Don't hesitate; waiting is what brought us to the unpleasant situation we find ourselves in now," the president urged. "We will strike these damned creatures before they have time to escape New York. We won't wait for them this time by setting up roadblocks, no; we will choose the time and place to strike, ourselves!"

"And what happens if we lose?" Once more someone raised that damned question.

"I want none of you thinking like that. Only know that we are doing our best and what we choose is the best solution, even if it doesn't prove to be a winning one." Clive said, and tried to believe his own words.

"So, 70% of our forces, right? All at one place, New York! Who could imagine!" the Secretary of Defense said absently, as though fascinated by the idea that all the war machines would be gathered in one place. Envisioning such an incredible scene was impossible.

"Mr. President, what about the nuclear strike on Buenos Aires?" an officer still seated at his desk asked.

"It proceeds as scheduled," one of the councilors said, looking at Clive with a look that didn't leave Clive any room to disagree.

The president nodded-he couldn't do otherwise. That movement turned something on inside him, a fire he couldn't quench. At that moment, it felt like a hydrogen bomb was exploding inside Clive's body, releasing a wave that drifted through his thoughts and feelings and burned them like they were dead leaves. Leaves of a dead tree, in a dead city...

THE LAST HOPE

They were all there: 70% of the American armed forces gathered in one spot, taking an entire day to surround the vast city of New York. The government had managed to call up the greatest military force that had ever been gathered in history. Half of them would evacuate Jersey City, where the predators had landed and conquered the area, while the other half would take over the Bronx. The predators hadn't attempted to spread any more and they seemed content to hold that area for the time being.

That day, there wasn't a single man who didn't believe, even for a second, that the human forces had the advantage, that humanity would turn out the victor. They all also knew that if they didn't make it that morning, they were never going to. But the sight of such an army, in full armament, that could easily cover all of Manhattan, gave courage even to the most pessimistic!

They were almost ready. The only thing they waited for was the order to charge into the area inhabited by the predators and exterminate even the smallest in their nests. The attack would begin first at Jersey City.

Some scattered attacks had occurred upon those units waiting in the direct line of attack; already over twenty deaths had been reported. But those incidents were for the most part instigated by deinonychus, animals that didn't hunt cooperatively, like velociraptors. Individual predators attacked the soldiers, knocking some of them down, before they were killed. In one of these attacks, a deinonychus was captured for the first time, but there wasn't enough time to study it and discover the creatures' weaknesses.

Nothing, not even these occasional attacks, prepared anyone for what would follow!

The field radio signaled and a soldier picked up the receiver. "This is operation 'Man's Nail'."

"I'm going to go shaving."

"Code accepted, sir," the soldier responded to the Defense Secretary. "At your command!"

"My orders are very simple, soldier. Advance at the double in twenty seconds!"

"Yes, sir! Anything else?"

"No. Put the countdown over the speakers. I want you to go in all together-don't leave any escape route to the damned animals. Now, go!"

The countdown was already issuing from the speakers, and the hearts of those there and elsewhere beat time. Twenty seconds passed before the greatest moment in the history of mankind. To some it felt like centuries!

The word "attack" sounded equally magic and promising to everyone. The first line of troops advanced on Jersey City. As they advanced they frequently lifted their guns and blew to pieces many of the predators foolish enough to attack them. The sight of the bleeding animals convulsing in the streets encouraged the fighters and made them believe even more in the victory they dreamt of.

Of course, the slaughter to follow would have nothing to do with these random incidents! The heart of the predators' territory was Manhattan, and that wasn't going to fall into their hands easily, no matter how many guns were turned against it!

The closer they got to Jersey City, the more intense a strange stench in the air became. Some of more experienced soldiers knew very well where the smell came from, but they preferred not to think about it. Those younger and older soldiers there that day to spill blood knew very well that, on the battleground, there would be scattered the bodies of their fellow countrymen who hadn't had the chance for a quick death by bullet or poison. A weapon is defined by how much pain it inflicts, not by the speed with which it kills!

They would soon enter the core area of Jersey City. Tall buildings rose around them, forcing many squads of soldiers to fall out to check the buildings and clear them of predators. Many of those squads never came back, but neither did the predators that had lived in those buildings-because the next step performed by the endless army wasn't to send more people inside, no. The order was specific. They were to set fire to the entire building.

Many buildings were torched, and most of the predators remained inside the buildings and burned alive, aware of what awaited them if they tried to escape. Some of the little velociraptors dashed from the tall buildings, their flesh scorched or still smoldering, only to fall with over thirty bullet holes in their bodies.

None of the soldiers ever felt sorry for those little creatures. If they were allowed to live, they would develop into ruthless killers, just like their parents!

In the meantime, the head of army had advanced a few miles, clearing the area they passed through, while the bulk of the army was still entering Jersey City, since the mass of war machines and soldiers easily covered the whole area! The real war was yet to begin.Millions of people and thousands of tanks had descended upon the streets of Jersey City, giving back to the city what it had been deprived of for so many hours: movement, life. The velociraptors didn't make any organized attempts to attack, at least for the time being, allowing the army to gain ground that they had held. But the situation was to change dramatically.For a moment, those watching the army's progress on their televisions saw this rather beautiful sight and believed that time had stopped. How else could they explain the sudden halt of the troops and tanks and the sudden silence? All the soldiers who were on the first line of attack had stopped walking, but why?

A terrible smell of rotting flesh had wormed into the soldiers' nostrils, disgusting them as never before in their lives. But it wasn't just that. That was nothing compared to the gruesome scene they saw in front of them! Some painter had taken a paintbrush made of human bones and hair, had diluted blood into tears and with that, had painted a picture straight out of a sick, dangerous imagination! Nowhere else would they see such a sight, not even in their worst nightmares-if they ever managed to sleep again.

A mountain range of dead people, some bodies intact, others torn in half, rose like a wall in front of them, as if telling them "this is as far as you go!" No one had ever imagined that so many could have died, no report spoke of anything of such magnitude. The mound of bodies didn't end, it wound among the buildings and beyond. It was longer than the front line of the army halted in front of it, and rose waist-high. The predators had gathered all the dead bodies and bones and brought them here, to set the boundaries of the area that they believed belonged to them!

When this was reported to the War Room, the order was immediate: "Go on." But something inside every soldier whispered that violation of the boundaries set by the predators would mean only death to those who dared to cross. The wall of half-eaten bodies was a warning, a sign to whoever crossed it that they would very soon belong to the predators!

The soldiers couldn't do otherwise; they couldn't lose courage and retreat. They slowly walked to the wall, covering their noses and trying not to look at the scattered limbs and the lifeless, blood-encrusted bodies any more than they had to. They didn't like the thought that they could very soon end up in a similar condition, but that wasn't enough to abort their mission.

As they approached they saw millions of flies humming above the dismembered bodies, making more noise than the army. The soldiers in front pulled up their hoods and got down to the horrible job of opening a hole in the human wall.

It was hard to tell whether the lead soldiers managed to lay their shovels on the dead bodies before they themselves dropped, decapitated, onto the wall of the dead, increasing its height even more.

The predator that dared to attack an entire army dropped dead as well, but before it died it had already taken three people with it. That incident shook everyone up; no one else was willing to try to clear the wall. They all knew that somewhere back there, more dangerous animals were hiding.

They soon found a solution, and, although they didn't like it much, it was the only one that would keep everyone alive. Two tanks immediately rolled forward there, and at other places along the wall. The men made room for them to pass, then watched the tanks level the wall in a shower of human blood. No predator attempted to stop the tanks, maybe because they knew that trying would be futile.

The human wall fell, revealing behind it a world where the streets were redder than usual, emptier than ever before. The two tanks that crossed over, having opened a passage, stopped and waited for the troops and the rest of the machinery to pass hesitantly through the crushed flesh of their fellow humans. Many threw up, but no one misinterpreted it as weakness. Little by little, the soldiers passed through the nine-foot-wide passage they had opened, each one concentrating on where to step and trying not to faint. No one wanted to think about the fact that, by entering the area, they were violating the ground the predators claimed to be theirs.

And then it happened.

Within moments, the streets were flooded with velociraptors and blood. Soldiers dropped dead one after the other. Every predator killed at least five soldiers before it crawled, dying, down the road. All of the creatures together were more dangerous than the soldiers had ever imagined when they'd been facing isolated incidents. It was too late now to withdraw; they couldn't go back! No matter how heavy the casualties were, what happened that day was their last chance; they couldn't lose.

The soldiers fought with everything they had, aiming their weapons directly at the animals' heads which, considering the speed of the animals, was almost impossible. However, the predators couldn't dodge the enemy's bullets forever. The humans had forgotten their shock at sight of the wall. Now they looked only ahead, toward battle!

Screams filled the air. Occasionally, scattered phrases of encouragement were heard:"Get them, brothers!"

" Rip their guts out; blow their brains away!"

"Don't leave even one alive!"

"Do you like sucking it now, you damned creature?"

Strangely enough, the scene fit the soldiers' cries. They were winning! The humans were much more numerous, incredibly more numerous, and the predators had begun realizing that, and making the first moves toward retreat. For the first time in the war, human were emerging as the victors!

The image the TVs portrayed showed clearly soldiers pursuing predators, instead of the other way around. The front line had penetrated nearly six hundred feet beyond the human wall, holding formation as they filled the streets.

Unfortunately, a very big mistake was about to be made.

In most cases, those in the front line of the enormous military force made the mistake, reacting to the predators' retreat, of advancing further down the wide streets. The predators lurking in the tall buildings around them sprang on them and tore them into pieces. Velociraptors jumped from the windows of the buildings that hadn't been checked yet and the soldiers found the enemy amongst them. That mistake cost thousands of lives and could have cost humanity its survival if more had followed them.

Those soldiers who had been behind the front line a little earlier were now in the line of fire. The street they walked down as they pushed the predators back was now filled with the dead bodies of their comrades. The sight was hard but the need for survival was stronger. They turned their hearts into stone and kept fighting for the sake of those still alive.

In the meantime, the predators' resistance was growing stronger, despite the army's advance deep into the city. They weren't far from the ultimate moment when they would trap the predators with the sea at their back. There, according to their orders, they would stop their vehicles and set the ordnance they had. This time the ring they would created on that side, facing Manhattan, would be impenetrable!

The soldiers observed a beautiful sight, no matter how much bloodshed had brought them to it: the last velociraptors standing in front of them didn't stay to fight. They turned and ran to the sea now visible between the buildings, in an attempt to escape from the huge army closing in on them. Their retreat turned into a rout!

Those soldiers who had gone there hoping to leave as winners started screaming with joy. They started running too, hunting the animals that had hunted their families. The whole army advanced at the double, since there was nothing left behind them to deal with. In a while they reached the coast.

There they discovered where the surviving animals were going. The damned creatures waded into the sea and swam as fast as they could, with only their heads out of the water, toward Manhattan. The creatures knew that there, surrounded by broad rivers, it would be very difficult for the humans to attack them. But, what they didn't know was that humanity, so infuriated by the creatures' terrible deeds, would tear down an entire city like Manhattan, just to get rid of them.

A few soldiers fired aimless shots into the water and then a celebration followed! The animals had been beaten this time and humanity tasted the sweetness of victory. That morning, all of mankind celebrated around the carcass of a dead deinonychus. For both Australians and North Americans, the outcome of that battle made them believe that nothing was lost. Jersey City was just the beginning!

But the news that brought the people real confidence came a bit later, when an equally powerful force attacked the predators in the Bronx. There too, the army encountered a wall of human remains; they followed the same tactics; but there, the only foes they met were about ten deinonychuses, no more. The velociraptors had already escaped and returned to Manhattan. They knew that the human forces were much more powerful than they were this time, they knew they couldn't play with them!

FATAL CONGRATULATIONS

"Congratulations, Mr. President; my deepest congratulations," the Secretary of Defense said. He shook the hand of his friend and colleague, obviously relieved. He didn't know why, but the president was reluctant to release his hand, as if he worried that this happiness, which came at the most appropriate moment, would say good-bye to them later. The Secretary had to slide his hand from between the sweaty hands of the president in order to release it.

"You look very happy, Clive!"

"I shouldn't be," he said without hesitation as a wide smile broke over his face.

"Of course you should. The last hours have offered us many things. Maybe you haven't considered it all; let me remind you-"

"There's no need to…"

"But no, let me-I also enjoy hearing them," the Secretary said and laughed. "Above all, we've managed to drive the animals away from the continental United States, something that we would only see in our dreams, after the debacle at the escape from Manhattan! Apart from that, we've managed to isolate the predators in two places that are, in fact, islands! I mean Manhattan and Long Island of course."

"In Sydney we also had something similar to an island at first, but then-"

"Come on, don't be a pessimist. Besides, we know that the animals in Manhattan will run out of food soon, because they were stupid enough to collect their food at some sort of wall, I think they said. I didn't understand much of that..." And of course he hadn't understood, because if he had even dared to imagine what the soldiers had seen with their eyes, then he wouldn't dare to call the dead body of a child "food!"

"I know, I know!"

"Good! Well, after the animals' stupidity there, they will begin starving. And don't forget that the damned things are great eaters! They'll have to seek food outside Manhattan, and you know what's waiting for them there this time. Exhausted from swimming and lack of food as they'll be, we can hope for casualties of one to two!" The Secretary referred to the average human losses that every predator would exact. "It's perfect, I'm telling you! Everything is perfect!"

"You got excited too soon. Have you forgotten Long Island and the other two cities? What's going to happen with them?" Clive said as his expression grew sad.

"But, we've found a solution for those, too. Have you forgotten already? Clive, the hydrogen bombs will do a much better job than the marines. You can count on that. And we won't have any human casualties!"

"You mean American casualties."

"Of course that's what I mean. Can you imagine how many young people would be lost if we decided to send reinforcements into those areas?"

"So instead of that, we will kill the people that live next to us!"

"I can't understand you."

"That's best. Pretend this conversation never happened," Clive snapped.

"No problem. One way or the other, the two of us will probably fall from the heights we've climbed together when this tragedy is over."

"I know," Clive said, "but something inside me is telling me that our positions aren't the only things we're going to lose!"

The War Room was filled with happy, smiling people-victorious people. That horrible worry, that terrible noise that upset and frightened people every time someone called out their name had now vanished. And despite their unbearable weariness, they were eager to work.

"Clive, Clive. Where were you, I've been looking for you!" Jackson, another member of the Congressional council said.

"To congratulate me, I suppose."

"But of course, although it's not just that."

"What happened, did trouble start again?" Clive asked with an apprehensive look.

"Not exactly, but the time is approaching!"

The president's expression changed, as if a black cloud had passed over it.

"You're talking about the nuclear strike. Why are you in such a hurry?"

"Stop the kibosh and come with me. It's time for the predators to get to know real Americans! Come on," Jackson insisted.

"I can't do otherwise!"

"It's good of you to finally realize that. come on, don't be long." Jackson walked ahead as if showing the way.

They walked to another, much smaller room. A large screen hung on the opposite wall. Right now, it showed two views. The first showed a map that included part of North America and Buenos Aires, while the other displayed a satellite image of the city. In the room were the government's most important members. Clive was the last one to arrive.

"Finally," one of the Senators said as he noticed the President crossing the room. The discussions stopped and everybody turned to look at Clive. "A little longer, and you would have missed the party!"

Clive didn't answer him. "What stage are you at?" he asked.

"Well, we're waiting for some information; specifically, we want to know how far the animals have spread."

"Why?"

"It's for safety matters. We want to be sure of how powerful the bomb should be."

"Add extra to the kilotons they decide upon. Since we're going to kill so many people, we should at least be sure of exterminating all the predators as well!" Clive said, and noticed that everyone stared at him strangely. "What's wrong? Why are you all looking at me like that?"

"Well, you spoke of kilotons, right?"

"Yes, but what does this have to do with-"

"It does Clive," the Secretary of Defense said. "You should know that fusion bombs-that is, hydrogen bombs-aren't measured in kilotons, but in megatons!"

Clive's eyes opened wide for a horrified moment. "How many megatons are you talking about?" he asked with difficulty.

"That's exactly what we want to find out," the Senator said. "That's what we're waiting for!"

A moment later the phone in the room started ringing. "It's them!" the Secretary of Defense said and headed towards the phone.

The power of the weapons under discussion-atomic fusion bombs-is phenomenal. One kiloton is equivalent to one thousand tons of dynamite, concentrated at one point. A thousand tons of dynamite in the same place can create a crater 270 feet in diameter and seventy feet deep. But of course, an atomic bomb possesses other goodies: a small size, and the release of radioactivity, which can ultimately cause even more human casualties.

But one kiloton doesn't seem to be enough to satisfy human ambition in terms of destructiveness. A bomb of 335 kilotons, the equivalent of 335 million kilograms of dynamite, could turn the 270-foot crater into one at least 1,800 feet wide. But that, too, isn't enough! It seems that today, we have to pass to the scale of megatons in order to start admiring our work.

One megaton, one billion kilograms of TNT-who can imagine the consequences it would have on nature, on man, on the entire world?

The Secretary of Defense was speaking in a low voice, with the phone tucked against his ear as if he didn't want anyone else to learn what he was listening to at that moment. He raised his head and tried to look into the eyes all of those who were anxiously waiting for a word from him.

"I don't have very good news," he said, but no one was surprised. And then he stammered, like a child that has forgotten how to speak from fear. He uttered a number. A very high number.

"Ten megatons!" he said.

Clive shut his eyes. He couldn't imagine using such power, even in his wildest nightmares!

"If we want to send just one bomb, which is recommended for various reasons, it should have a power of ten megatons," the Secretary of Defense repeated.

"How many of them do we have?" someone asked.

"Three or four, I don't remember. The important thing is that those bombs were never meant to be used!"

"Well, it seems they're going to be used after all!"

The Secretary of Defense nodded, seeming for once troubled.

Clive sat down, crushed by the unexpected turn of events. He remembered the dream he'd had, recalled the screams of the children, the side effects of the radioactive fallout, and he thought, "Oh my god, this is going to be a lot worse..."

The members of the government looked at each other for a while. Then one of them broke the silence, saying, "The decision has been made; we can't back down just because we're afraid of a large number!"

Some of those present agreed, some didn't say anything, but all were criminals!

Clive listened to it all, unable to do anything because of his involvement in the farm program. He raised his head and asked the Secretary of Defense a simple question. "What will be the consequences of the detonation of such a bomb in the center of Buenos Aires?"

The Secretary hesitated for a moment but he eventually answered. "Total destruction. The crater alone will be 6,500 feet wide. There will only be dust left, to a depth of over 500 feet. That, of course, depends on the height at which the bomb explodes-the height of burst, or HOB. They'll probably suggest we set it off at about 4,309 feet above the ground, where it will be most destructive."

"Most, most destructive? What do you mean by that?"

"I mean that nothing will survive within a range of four miles! Nothing at all! From that point on, the survival of predators underground is speculated, but..."

"But velociraptors won't have built any nests beyond four miles yet, right?"

"Right, Mr. President. From that point on, up to six miles, all animals that come in direct contact with the wave will be killed on the spot. Then again, if there are any in some buildings, not knowing how to protect themselves, they will be injured and will die within a few hours due to the radioactivity and the high temperatures. The course of the wave has been calculated theoretically and, if I remember well, it will last for about 17,235 seconds. I don't think they'll have enough time to get very far!" The Secretary of Defense stopped talking and took a deep breath. Then he noticed the strange and sad look on Clive's face.

"You've told me everything," Clive said, "but you didn't tell me the most important thing! How many people will die in that attack, Secretary? How many?"

The Secretary lowered his head while he made the calculations mentally. "It depends," he said. "It depends on the wind, the number of survivors; it depends on a lot of things."

"Can't you just give us a number?" Clive implored. Clive wanted all the people present to hear how many thousands, how many hundreds of thousands of people would suffer.

"No, I can't. I'm sorry."

"Why all this concern?" someone asked. "We will find out from the media ten minutes after the strike," he added, unconscious of what he was saying.

Most agreed with him. Since the nuclear attack was their only solution, they didn't have to deal with the meaningless numbers of human casualties. The supreme target was the elimination of the predators and that was something that was going to happen at any cost! But the tragic thing in all of this was that, in some way, all those people that had decided to kill in the name of mankind were right! No matter how many the human losses were, they would definitely be less than the entire population of earth.

"Now, as far as the city itself is concerned," the Secretary of Defense continued, "nothing will stay standing within a distance of three miles, while the buildings between three and four and a half miles, if they're still standing, will be ready to collapse. From that point on, there will be partially destroyed buildings."

"So, we're talking about a city-terminator!" someone exclaimed, unable to hide his excitement.

"And not just the city," the Defense Secretary said. "But now, since we've decided what to use and what effects it will have, I think it's time to start thinking about retaliation!"

Many people shifted in their seats. It was obvious that an attack with nuclear weapons, without any warning or any agreement, and even worse, with a hydrogen bomb that had only been used in tests, would cause great international turmoil.

"You're talking about a threat of war," Clive said, not at all surprised.

"Oh yes, that's exactly what I'm talking about!"

"'What can I say. As far as I know, it is rumored that China possesses nuclear bombs of one megaton, but that hasn't been ascertained..."

"Russia and Europe have the technology and the infrastructure; they definitely have the equipment as well!" the Secretary contributed to a dialogue that was developing exclusively between him and the president.

Clive held his head and said, "We've started a war with the predators and now we're in danger of starting a war with each other. Is that really what you prefer? What are you afraid of more, dinosaurs against man or man against man himself? Answer me!"

The Senators looked at each other. For the first time, they wondered if they really had to blow such a big city sky-high, now they would be threatened themselves.

Their hesitation disappeared with the words of an ambitious young Senator who said, "It can't be otherwise; it's the only solution to what is happening to us right now. Besides, if they want war, it won't be too difficult for us to respond..."

The Secretary of Defense answered immediately. "Of course, it will be difficult after so many losses due to our own internal problems in New York. Apart from that, don't forget that we've sent armed forces to other places on earth in order to help; forces that we don't have time to recall!"

"If they threaten us with war, which I doubt they'd do, we can drop a smaller hydrogen bomb on Manhattan, where everyone is already dead! That way, the other nations won't be able to claim that we've served interests contrary to those of all humanity!"

"It's all about interests, after all," Clive whispered.

"Clive," the Secretary of Defense said, "that word isn't as bad as it seems."

"Fuck him, he's just an asshole," someone in the room said suddenly. Clive stood up. "Who-"

"I did!" A Senator stepped forward. "And be careful of what you're going to say, Mr. President. Don't forget that all this is happening because of you and him." He pointed at the Defense Secretary.

Clive didn't say a word; what was there to say? Whatever he did, he was a murderer, out of negligence or otherwise didn't matter anymore, definitely not when the victims were so numerous. But the problem was, the victims were going to become even more numerous!

"Sit down and shut up!" the unkind young Senator, no more than a messenger of reality said. And reality was too harsh to be heard nicely from any mouth.

Clive harrumphed and sat down. He decided not to speak again in that council, since no one would listen to anything he said. He remained a mere observer, a witness to a sentence of death upon some hundreds of thousands of innocent people.

"So, we proceed without worrying whether or when foreign forces will threaten us," the Defense Secretary continued. "Europeans are not stupid, I know that very well. They will understand that, if we violated our treaty, we did so for the good of the world, not just for us. In God's name, we're the ones who are being sacrificed; they're not!" he shouted.

That phrase sounded so nice, so convincing. Now, if we asked him whether he would take the place of those who still lived around Buenos Aires and if he would accept that, well that's another, much greater issue...

Nevertheless, as anticipated, all the rest agreed with him, leaving the issue of reactions aside and focusing on organizing the mission they had assigned to themselves. Everything was going to happen in absolute secrecy and would end in a couple of hours. That was the amount of time left between the launch of the missile and the wound that would open on the surface of the earth. A wound of six and a half thousand feet...

COUNTDOWN

"Call the research center studying the samples one last time. See if they've found anything," the Secretary of Defense said. Clive wasn't in a position to speak.

The answer that came a minute later. "Nothing sir, they're still searching!" No one expected anything different, no one hoped…

"Let it be," the Secretary said. He sat down in front of the only computer in the room. No other officer knew the top-secret information he typed on its keyboard. In a few seconds he was connected with the nuclear missile control room. "They are waiting for us," he said, turning to those gathered.

"Are you saying that the ten Meg bomb is already ready?"

The Secretary nodded. "Very well. Does anyone have any objections before our precious killer is up in the sky?" he asked, but he knew that no one would react. Clive didn't speak!"

"This is the Secretary of Defense. You have approval to proceed," he said, so cold-heartedly, so painlessly, into the computer microphone. "I request you start countdown for the missile launch of the ten megaton fusion bomb in combination with nine more decoy missiles. I'm forwarding the authorizations from the five main controllers now." He started keyboarding a whole eighteen-digit code he had memorized. Then he pressed his finger onto a white plate that scanned his fingerprints. So did four more people, in a specific order that the president had been forced to disclose. The command was approved and the countdown soon began.

The members of the government looked at each other, worried. Some of them regretted their decision at that moment, but they didn't say so; they never spoke about it. Clive remained still in his place, keeping his head low, where it deserved to be. Time passed at the same pace it always does, never hesitating to move on to the next second. Perhaps a few tears trickled along with the seconds.

I'd like to wish that they did, although I believe that we are more ruthless than time itself. But somewhere there during the countdown, at 20, at 19, 18, 17, 16...somewhere there I was also confused and I didn't know what we were counting for anymore! Tears of a wound that was going dry on 15, 14, 13...? Or the last minutes of a life that was ending on 12, 11, 10, 9...

LIKE THE WIND THAT CONSTANTLY BLOWS...
LIKE THE SUN THAT RISES!

8, 7, 6, 5, 4, 3, 2, 1...

The missile now flew between the clouds; the atrocious killer was flying! And it was in view of the stars, though they didn't want to see it. Soon there wouldn't be any sky in which to see stars. It would be lost behind the dust, along with the hopes of the people who once lived under it. And no man would be able to do anything because beasts, real beasts this time, would have taken control!

The missile flew from north to south, on its way to kill hundreds of thousands, but only a dozen people had decided this fate. The hydrogen bomb, hidden among nine decoy missiles, would definitely reach its target and kill. It would kill not only the predators, but the humans that hadn't managed to leave as well, people that had been trapped in the city. Nothing would survive within a range of three and a half miles, nothing!

Missiles had also entered the airspace of other countries, but those controlling them had made sure that they would follow a course far away from the super-modern radar that would notice their nature. The U.S.A. simply said that they were sending air reinforcements to a random country, presenting the bombs as aircraft, something that no government bothered to confirm, or maybe didn't have the time to do. The truth was that, at that moment, there wasn't any sign of suspicion in people. This was the only moment in history when man faced a common enemy. But even at that moment, there was going to be exploitation.

Only seconds were left before the payload reached its destination. If those below knew that, they would have drawn away from the place of detonation, but even if they did, they couldn't have prevented it. Historical decision built on speculation and doubt, nothing more.

The Secretary of Defense had estimated it himself, but he hadn't said it, being unwilling to terrify his colleagues. You see, he wanted their decision to be based merely on the criterion of whether they should make a nuclear strike or not, and not on consideration of the power of that nuclear strike, which was an issue best left with the experts. So, the Secretary had estimated correctly that the explosion that was going to take place would have five hundred, yes five hundred, times more power than the strike at Hiroshima over fifty years ago! The bomb that was used then was the equivalent of the detonator on the present bomb!

No matter how many times more powerful it was, no one could stop it now, now that it was in the final stretch and was flying over Argentina. It passed over Santa Fe, Rosario and then it was above Buenos Aires. No one had suspected anything until the last twenty seconds. It was then that the U.S. stopped denying the abnormality that showed on radar, an abnormality that indicated that the aircraft weren't aircraft. By then, there wasn't enough time to shoot down even one of the ten bombs, one of which carried their death inside it.

A great flash, like a rising sun, and then a heat wave like the blowing wind.

The mushroom cloud rose once more, this time more powerful than ever! And exactly as they had predicted, the nearest buildings turned into dust; the earth opened and swallowed nests and people;

the wind became searing hot! The air this time wasn't flooded with the screams of people and animals, there wasn't time for that; the wave swept through much faster. Eighteen seconds, eighteen seconds of pain and anguish. That is how long the wave lasted; as long as they had predicted.

And the more the fire advanced, the more the mushroom cloud opened and spread over the dead city, the more it weakened. Now it did not kill instantly but made its victims suffer, covered by some red wall in a once living neighborhood. The velociraptors died that day, but so did humans; so did their conscience.

After the flash, after the shock wave, came darkness and polluted air. Thank God the wind blew towards the sea; thank God. Still, day turned into night for many days, and the wind didn't prevent the radioactivity from contaminating water and earth.

The sun was hidden behind the dust for many days, as if scared of facing the consequences of man's greed. If only that cloud of dust and radioactivity had never left that place to reveal a gigantic crater and, for a great distance beyond it, half-demolished, crumbling buildings. Even farther out, people contaminated by radioactivity had no hope of survival. Those who had been vaporized that day were lucky, very lucky!

After that entire scene had played itself out, some dared to believe that, yes humanity had made it. But, what, really, was it that we had made?

RESPONSIBILITIES

Those in the War Room looked, bewitched, at the satellite pictures on the large screen. On the electronic map, the shock wave seemed to have reached its end, swallowing velociraptors and people without exception, without anything. That's exactly what it left behind, a big nothing. This, some people were very proud of!

The nuclear blast of ten megatons had almost swallowed all of Buenos Aires but it hadn't stopped just at that, the predators hadn't been just there. The wave that could kill or fatally injure without throwing buildings down continued its course for a much greater distance. It traveled many miles and carved a red circle that was constantly becoming wider on the observation monitor. That was almost the only thing seen by those who had made the decision, a red circle.

The operation was completed successfully, at least for the U.S. The telephones rang constantly but no member of the government chose to speak for the time being. They had to decide what they would claim and what would be released to the press. Hard decisions were just beginning for them.

"Very nice," the Secretary of Defense said. Clive still wasn't speaking. "Now, going out of this room, we must all agree what it is that we know and what it is that we don't. Everything is as we've said, nothing is changed. I don't think I have to remind you that we have to hold our cards close when we're asked if there's going to be another attack like that!"

"Pay attention to what he's just said gentlemen!" a Senator called out. "The reporters out there are very clever and they will try to lead us into revealing more than we wish. We are only to give answers that we consider necessary, is that clear?"

They all agreed with the two men's words. The strike on Buenos Aires would be presented as an act of disaster relief, while the absence of warning was something necessary-no country would accept being bombed and showered with radioactivity. As far as retaliation was concerned, they would try to avoid that by saying that they would make a similar strike on Manhattan in the future, something that they hoped wouldn't be necessary.

In a few minutes, the White House was filled with reporters seeking members of the government. However, the government was in another building that had been kept away from public scrutiny; the White House was only a facade. For the time being, the reporters had to suffice with a few spare statements from representatives who at least didn't deny the participation of the American government in the incident. The official statements would be made on national TV later, by the president himself.

Yes, It Was Us!

He walked slowly, his legs feeling heavier than ever. He would get to the pressroom soon; he would get on the stand and say everything he wanted to say-no, he was going to say what he had been ordered by the others to say! And then the questions would come...

The reporters in the room all stood up, honoring the appearance of the president, of the murderer! He headed to his position behind the microphones and took a deep breath. The reporters sat down.

"The U.S.A. accepts responsibility for the incident. We accept responsibility and are ready to answer to any question that doesn't violate top government secrets. But, before you start asking questions, I'd like to tell you what we know, and answer what you would probably like to ask."

The reporters took out their notebooks and the cameras focused on his face.

"There wasn't any warning for the simple reason that, if we sat down to talk about it, we would have lost too much valuable time. We wouldn't have gotten anywhere. The reaction of Argentina confirms this. Besides, the issue is global and it had to be resolved on a global level. Because, if the predators spread further, then they wouldn't have harmed only Argentina, but the rest of the world as well.

"Apart from that, the destructive power of the bomb that was used was the lowest possible for the total elimination of our enemy. It might be a frightening sight, and it might remind you of past mistakes, but this has nothing to do with those! Weapons don't merely kill; they also save. And in this case, the weapon killed a few thousand but saved many billions! I'm sure that everyone would make the same decision we did!"

The reporters raised a wave of questions, less damning than the one Clive had answered but equally painful. The president pointed at one of them.

"How great were the human losses due to the bomb?" the reporter asked.

"We don't know..."

"You mean you didn't know even before you launched the missile? But that's-"

"I mean we don't now exactly!" Clive retorted.

"Then tell us approximately."

"If you really must know, over 600,000!"

"Thank you very much, Mr. President," the reporter said and sat down again.

The rest of them, as if forgetting where they were, didn't rise from their seats and immediately try to speak. But they didn't hesitate for long. "How many times more powerful than the one at Hiroshima was this bomb?"

Clive cleared his throat. "About five hundred times more powerful."

"And, is it true that the bomb you dropped has never been used under real conditions?"

"It was a hydrogen bomb, ma'am, but I can't tell you anything more!"

Another reporter jumped up without having been addressed, saying, "How many kilotons were used?"

"You weren't addressed!" Clive protested.

"How many kilotons, Mr. President?" the reporter repeated.The question put Clive in a difficult position. "Ten megatons, sir; are you happy now?"

Some didn't understand what that number meant but they realized the difference between kiloton and megaton. The president pointed at another reporter.

"How many victims of the radioactive fallout will there be?"

"Thank God, there won't be too many. The wind was blowing to the sea."

"And as far as retaliation is concerned, how do you intend to handle the issue?"

"Not the way I'm handling it with you," Clive said and laughed. Some probably wondered how he had the courage to do that. The drugs he had been given before the press conference had definitely helped. "Let's get serious now. What we did was count the victims on both sides, no matter how horrible it might sound. We concluded that it's to mankind's advantage to drop a hydrogen bomb and kill a few thousand people who were probably doomed anyway. Doing so saved all of you, and even more people. Now, just two more questions, please; no more than that."

Another woman spoke. "Why didn't you do the same thing with Manhattan?"

Clive wished he had never addressed her. "Manhattan is a different case. We have trapped the predators there and they will soon starve to death. It's a whole different case!"

"You could simply have said that it hurts more when it's one of your own cities," she said, and Clive realized that he had addressed a reporter from Argentina.

"Another question?" he said to the others, ignoring her.

"Mr. President, will you use the same tactic with Australia?"

"The answer to that is top-secret. If you will excuse me now..." Clive quickly left the room. Many questions were shouted after him, some hard ones, other inhumane ones, making him run even faster. This time the wave of rage and shame was directed at the ones who were to blame and only them! The time had come for them to pay, and the price would be so high that they would one day wish they had perished in the blast of the hydrogen bomb!

DAILY NEWSPAPER TITLES

Hundreds of thousands dead, and the president is laughing!
500 times more guilty!
Man; is that the real enemy?
War: threat, or something more?
Where is the city?
Suicide!
Third World War!
The real end!
For mankind...
The articles don't matter anymore now...But one article, one particular paragraph, is really worthy of our attention. That article was titled...

Velociraptors, the children of a president!
"The information is unconfirmed; nothing that we report below necessarily represents the truth. However, our sources have lead us to believe that whatever we do, we cannot keep it to ourselves, no matter how gruesome the facts are. Besides, the truth is always gruesome!

"We won't keep our secret until the end of the article; no, this is a special case where you have the right to know from the start. According to our informants, it is believed that the president both concealed and participated in the production of the predators!"

"There is no mistake; we wrote the sentence you've just read knowing full-well the consequences of our deeds. We know what it means the same way we know the effect that it's going to have. But, ladies and gentlemen, believe us, we would never have written it if the evidence weren't so incriminating and so solid! We must preserve the anonymity of our informants, but we will make public as much as possible."

The article went on for many pages. The writer stated facts and added lies every now and then to impress readers more. But the allegation on which the article was based was true, and something that could irreparably shake the entire government at a time when all the other countries were pressing for retaliation because of the immoral attack launched by the United States.

THE PUNISHMENT

Clive read the newspaper article containing his obituary that, unfortunately for him, would soon be in every house in America and later all over the world. The end had come much earlier than he had expected. There was nothing he could do anymore. The investigations into his history would grow numerous and everything that had been buried for all those years would surface. God only knew what the reaction would be!

He sat alone in one of his luxurious offices that didn't have anything to offer him anymore. He knew he was guilty, that he deserved the worst. But he couldn't wait. The passage of time was torture for him. Guilt burned like fire in his soul, a fire that could not be put out. The moment had come when he wished he'd died with those he'd killed.

His face was sweaty. A few tears mingled with the sweat, too few in comparison to the people that had died. There was nothing he could do to make it up, no lost life would ever come back. And even if some did survive the tragedy he had created, with what courage would he face the rage and pain of the relatives of those lost? Death was beginning to seem an absolutely logical solution to his tired mind; the only thing that was left was for his body to follow as well.

He wept. He couldn't hold the pain inside him anymore. He cried for the lives he had taken, lives like his own, which he was determined to take soon. He leaned over and slowly pulled the handle on his desk drawer. The gun now lay in front of him.

He looked at it like a young man facing a naked girl for the first time. He had the same look, exactly the same. After a while, the young man took courage and Clive took the gun in his hands. He fell in love with the barrel of the gun from the first moment, because he knew that it would give him the ticket to a magic world, far away from his responsibilities, close to his sweetheart.

Gently stroking her body, he brought the gun up to his head. He was one step away from freedom.

He remembered the dream he'd had earlier; he remembered the dreams he'd had as a child. They had nothing to do with what he was now living. He remembered his first love and then, then he remembered the hydrogen bomb, the great cataclysm, and suddenly he didn't want to remember anymore!

The next day, the press wrote about the death of the American president, Bennett Clive. No one mourned for him; no one in the whole world.

WAITING...

They had nowhere to go; there was nothing they could do to save their lives. They looked at the army concentrated around Manhattan and they wished they could fly to the other side of the city. Daniel, Nancy and Clara were among those who hadn't made it out, and hadn't had time to call for help. They'd sought help from the rooftop of a sky-scraper but there was never any given to them.

Minutes passed, the quietest minutes of their lives. Three people together in one place, and none of them spoke. They preferred to watch the troops gathered around the city that was now their jail. They wondered why the troops didn't attack, but deep inside they knew that something like that would have devastating consequences because the ground, or even more so the sea, wasn't on their side!

The helicopters had stopped flying over their heads, no longer searching for survivors. Finding survivors after so many days would be nothing short of a miracle, and there are no miracles in our times. If Clara and Nancy and Daniel had thought of going to the rooftop earlier, they might have made it in time, but not anymore.

Nancy huddled in a corner, disturbed by the cold. Daniel hadn't taken his eyes from the endless army that was too far away to help them. Clara had knelt and was crying inconsolably for their abandonment, for her mistakes, for everything.

"They will never come to help us mum, right?" Nancy asked without raising her gaze from the ground. She didn't have to look to know that her mother was crying.

"They will come, my child, they will," Clara said unconvincingly. "Don't you see the army that has gathered outside the city? They're here for us, to help us."

"And why are they so late mum?" Nancy asked in a quavering voice.

"They have other jobs to do too, sweetheart. We're not the only ones."

"Maybe they haven't seen us yet. That's it, if we start a fire they'll see us!" Nancy exclaimed.

Daniel shook his head. "The velociraptors will also see us, and trust me, they'll be the first to come before our own," he said and then added in such a low voice that he was the only one to hear, "if any of our own ever come!"

Hours passed and no one could find a subject worthy of their last moments to talk about. Clara and the children had discussed only meaningless, hollow topics. Now that time was short and counting against them, they had nothing to talk about that would make their last moments special. Instead, they allowed silence to make those last moments even more excruciating. Each spoke to their own conscience, the only real and serious conversation that humanity has ever managed.

On deeper consideration it arises that today's culture came up from that conversation, only man prefers to call it thinking and meditation rather than conversation, so as not to degrade it. Unfortunately, degradation came from somewhere we didn't expect, from human feelings; that's what guilt actually is!

In the meantime, the sun was beginning to set, taking its precious light with it and leaving darkness to prevail. The children, like all children, were afraid of the dark and that night was no different, or was it? That night, before the sun set, the kids weren't afraid of the dark but were terrified that the sun would set. The light was so beautiful that they didn't want to lose sight of it for a second, knowing that those moments might be their last ones.

The sunset that day seemed much brighter and much more special. It was the same sun that had climbed the sky the previous day; it was the people that had changed. And only the sight of death could change people!

Nancy wondered why God didn't let her live first and then judge her. She couldn't come up with an answer that satisfied her. Then she considered that some people live and kill because they like killing during their lives. And in the end, they end up not deserving the life they've been given. They die ashamed or perhaps honored; what matters is not whether they're honored or shamed, but that they have already lived! Time will never come back for them, they lived and abused the gift they had been given, the gift they decided to deprive others of.

Daniel, on the other hand, wasn't bothered by whether he deserved this end or not. For Daniel there was no end. He looked constantly at the horizon, dazzled. The light was the only thing he would miss when he lost his life.

He remembered his father, who was so often traveling that Daniel had hardly known him. He remembered the death of his stepmother, and for a moment his eyes filled with tears. The tears trickled quickly down his cheeks and were gone leaving nothing behind but a bunch of memories that would soon be lost, too, as if they'd never existed.

Both children, helplessly in love with each other, didn't manage to live together and share their existence and their consciousness. Death was coming for both of them at the same time; but they couldn't cry for the life of someone who was going to leave, even if that someone was the one they loved! Fate didn't give them the time, and they didn't have the courage. They had lost one of the most precious of human feelings; to die loving someone else.

That wasn't all they would lose. The sun was sliding behind a few clouds on the horizon, painting the sky a reddish color preparatory to a night that was going to be painted red, one way or the other.

Nancy stood up and went to stand next to Daniel. A smile lightened the boy's face for a moment, but it was soon gone. Together they looked at the sun that was half set, and then took each other's hand. They closed their eyes for a moment, wishing to see what the darkness was like that waited for them, but they opened them very soon. Oh my God; life was so wonderful!

THE SECOND DECISION

The news of the president's death hardly surprised the other members of the government. Maybe they had also considered, as he had, that suicide would be the best solution at this point. The source of the information leak was never discovered. The government went on, without losing any other member. Strangely enough, the part the Secretary of Defense had played in the "farm" was kept secret.

Vice-president Foster accepted Clive's vacant post with great sorrow, or so he said. Now, there was no one in power who would hesitate to use nuclear weapons, even after what had happened.

But the atmosphere that had been created required a re-evaluation of the entire situation. That was something the new President didn't neglect to do. Soon after assuming his new duties, he called for convocation of the Congressional council. Half an hour later, all the council members were present in the round room.

"A detailed report on the situation, please," the new president said, savoring his power.

A man stood up. "One of the three disaster areas, Buenos Aires, has been completely annihilated. No predator has survived and we believe that the underground nests have collapsed due to the earthquake caused by the explosion."

"Go on…"

"Sydney has turned into a giant nest of predators. They hatch and spread from there in all directions, infecting other towns and villages within a range of many miles. In that part of the world, the predators have spread more than anywhere else. For some mysterious reason, perhaps pertaining to the climate, velociraptors prefer to constantly roam. The situation there has nothing in common with Buenos Aires, or I should say, the former Buenos Aires!"

And New York, what's the situation there?"

"There's nothing dramatically new there. The two species of predators, velociraptors and deinonychuses, are trapped in Manhattan, unable to spread to the continent. Unfortunately, they have managed to reach Long Island as well, but they haven't created a settlement there; they are merely present. However, there's an enormous migration expected shortly, towards the only open route-Long Island-when their food supply is gone. For some strange reason, perhaps a desire to dominate the entire North American continent, they tend to move towards the continent rather than towards Long Island. But now they won't have any other choice unless they want to starve to death."

"Very nice; now, how can we take advantage of the expected breakout to Long Island?"

"We can't. We haven't got the results of the research on the farm's records yet, and we probably won't have them in time. You see; many problems have come up because of the great security and secrecy of the project. The computer experts are having trouble decoding the data and the biologists are in an even worse situation!"

"I think I have something to suggest," someone said, "but it would be very difficult, perhaps even unfeasible."

"You're free to say it; at this point, even a crazy idea may grant us victory!" President Foster said.

"Well, we know that the predators will attempt to escape and will all move to the other end of the East River, right?"

"Right!"

"So, what we have to take advantage of is the fact that the animals will be forced to swim for a long period of time."

"And how can we take advantage of that?"

"It's very simple. By throwing a very powerful biological poison into the water at that moment!"

A silence spread throughout the room. Everyone looked thoughtful. Something like that could, indeed, work!

"Go on."

"I have nothing more to say, Mr. President. Both you and I know that the currents in those areas are not very strong and the poison will have enough time to take effect. In addition, we avoid polluting the air of our environment. I'm telling you that this is a unique chance; we must take advantage of it!"

"And what kind of poison is it that kills merely on contact?"

"Waterproof particles of the O variation sir; that's what it's called. It doesn't kill on contact but upon entering the lungs; it has a high level of success."

Some in the room had taken deep breaths upon hearing "poison."

"And what effect will it have on us; can it be carried beyond the sea?"

"The effects it will have on us will come much later, when the substance spreads to areas where people fish. But-and I want you to listen to this carefully-those waterproof particles can't escape into the atmosphere where they would be more dangerous than ever!"

"I like the solution you're offering," Foster said. "That way, we will avoid nuclear attack and the radioactivity that would pollute our ground. In that way, the effect will disperse around the entire world and will be lessened!"

"Exactly" the great inventor of the wonderful idea said, and laughed.

"Is there any countermeasure that could decrease the effectiveness of the poison after its use?" someone else asked, obviously worried.

"None available."

"At least we could set up barriers to prevent its spread…"

"No, we will lose valuable time. Let it spread into the entire ocean; its effectiveness will be minimized and there won't be any serious problems," Foster said, disregarding every rule of morality towards nature. But who thought of nature when there were other problems to think of. "How long will it take for the poison to take effect?"

"It depends on the time it will take to spread in the water. Special machines will see to its immediate spread; the predators won't even make it to the opposite coast!"

"It sounds nice," the president said, "but are those...those particles of the O variation so effective as to kill such an animal at once?"

The schemer laughed. "Oh yes, they are very powerful," he said.

The new weapon that was rooted in biology, the same scientific field that had given birth to the predators, was considered much more effective because it didn't kill people-at least, not immediately. The delay was of great importance to the government; random incidents that arose later would not be attributed to the spread of the particles. The particles were actually alive, with a short lifespan that would eliminate evidence of their fatal effects. But that didn't apply if the weapon contaminated fish!

The O variation was far more dangerous than it sounded. The Biopreparat program, which had been renamed rather than terminated as it was supposed to have been, had studied the O variation with great interest. Its destructive effect on every kind of organism had triggered new ideas for the development of weapons that didn't destroy an entire city in order to kill its habitants. This was a new kind of stealthy strike. The hydrogen bomb seemed primitive in comparison to a particle that, in the lungs of an animal, led to certain death.

The order had been given to prepare for the use of the O variation. The council dealt with some other, less important issues, and was about to adjourn, but it didn't.

A man of about middle age barged through the door and ran into the room to stop, short of breath, before the president. The guards tried to stop him but the president signaled them to leave him alone. It seemed the man had something very important to say, something that didn't appear good at all.

"Thank you, Mr. President," the man said, taking a deep breath.

"Don't thank me, but tell me quickly, what made you run in here in such a way?"

"The news, sir, the horrible news!"

"What are you talking about?"

"Two, Mr. President, there are two ills that are knocking on our door!"

"God damn it, speak up!"

"Calm down, Mr. President; what you have to hear requires calmness. It's about retaliation; there was a threat!"

"A threat made by whom?"

"By Argentina, but Russia and half of Europe backs them up! There's a war coming sir, a world war!"

"What are you talking about? You're definitely exaggerating."

"Maybe I am, but they've made it clear! We have to exterminate the predators within eight hours! Otherwise…"

"Otherwise what?"

"Otherwise they will strike, Mr. President; they will strike with a ten megaton bomb!"

"Where?"

"But, I though I told you. New York, of course-that's where they'll strike!"

"But it can't be," Foster stammered. It felt like the whole earth was moving under him. "Ten megatons is much more than what's required!"

"I don't know about that, but that's what they said and they're not negotiating over it!"

The face of the new president went red with rage and indignation. But he couldn't do anything against the other countries. They had justice on their side and they also had the power. There was nothing he could do.

"But it's not just that!" the unfortunate messenger said. The president looked at him, terrified, as if he couldn't imagine what could be worse. "Australia..." the man said "...it seems that the predators have escaped from Australia! An entire nest was found at Quezon, in the Philippines, and another, bigger one at Bangkok. They are in continental Asia!"

Everything was lost. They had hardly managed to deal with the animals in New York, and two more infestations had appeared in two other cities! Maybe they would have to bomb the entire world after all; maybe that was the only solution!

No one in the room spoke. The messenger drew away and left them to think and seek a solution.

"We must leave Asia to its fate," the president said suddenly. "We must focus on our own problem!"

"Maybe, if they find out what happened in Australia, it will give us more time!" someone said.

"Our negotiators will see to that, but I don't think we can count on it. The O variation will be used today; we will release it in the air over the city!"

The man who had suggested its use in the water a while earlier stood up and shouted, "That can't happen, that's inhumane!"

"Inhumane towards whom?"

"Towards the survivors, the neighboring communities, man!"

"There are no survivors anymore; the neighboring communities are already evacuated, and for those that are not, I will make sure that they are emptied in the next few hours!"

"We will never make it..."

"Maybe you have something better to offer than the nuclear bomb they are threatening us with. Fuck, people see nothing more than explosions! If we adopt the same method we used for Buenos Aires for New York, we'll be buried under tons of mud! Biological weapons are far more efficient!"

"And far more painful, Mr. President," the other man added.

"May God rest their souls," Foster said and was through with his conscience and the concerns he had undertaken. He asked if anyone had any objections. They all agreed; they couldn't see any other viable solution that wouldn't destroy them as politicians!

But the man who had originally suggested using the O variation lowered his head and uncharacteristically said, "The O variation in water is a different scenario than using it in the air, an entirely different scenario!"

No one gave him any notice; the case was closed. The plan was followed to the letter. Within a short time, most of the tanks and soldiers had been withdrawn from the area around Manhattan while those that stayed behind were equipped with special isolation suits to prevent them from being affected by the particles. The O variation would only harm unprotected organisms, and it wouldn't be able to go from one animal to the other, because it wasn't contagious. There was no fear of an epidemic.

The experts armed a remote-controlled F22 with the equipment required to release the lethal particles as dust that would scatter in the wind, scattering death everywhere.

NOTHING TO FORGET...

Darkness had fallen over Manhattan. A few stars were visible in the sky, while the moon sometimes hid behind the black clouds and sometimes revealed its white light. No house had its lights on; the power supply had been cut off. No cars traveled the dangerous streets; nothing was left as a reminder of the world that had been familiar for so many years. Everyone was gone; some because they had escaped in time; others because they didn't make it in time and were now lying somewhere, silent and still. The only lights visible were the lights of the military vehicles and the lights of the other districts, of Jersey and Brooklyn and the others.

Now, for some strange reason, the lights of the vehicles were beginning to move-they were leaving!

Clara was the first one to notice their movement, and consequently the movement of the people, too. Her mind filled with terrible thoughts that weren't far from truth. Exactly then, she realized who their real enemy was.

"Kids, kids, wake up," she shouted desperately, nudging Daniel and Nancy, who had just managed to get to sleep.

"What's going on?" Daniel asked.

"They're leaving; the military forces are going away!"

"They're what?" Nancy asked.

"They're going away, my daughter! I'm sure they're up to something! In God's name, will they try to kill the creatures without considering the human losses?"

"What, what?" Daniel said, as he opened his eyes. "But, that can't be happening, it can't happen!"

"There's no other explanation for this sudden withdrawal, is there!"

Daniel looked in that direction and tried to think. He wasn't long in understanding that Clara was right.

"We must show them we're here, alive, at any cost, even if that means that the predators will detect us. We'll be ready!" Clara said, bringing Nancy's idea back up. "If we start a fire and make signals-I don't know! Maybe they would make it in time to pick us up before the predators find us!"

The two kids seemed troubled. They soon realized that Clara was right. Besides, if those in power had decided to strike with a weapon of massive destruction, they shouldn't just sit around and wait. They definitely had to do something, even if it was risky!

Within a few minutes, they'd climbed down a few floors, gathering wood and anything that could be burned. In the moonlight, Daniel saw a lighter on a table of the restaurant. Its owner must have forgotten it there when he'd been informed of the special events taking place in Central Park a few days ago.

Paper soft drink cups, files from offices, broken chairs, almost everything could be useful. In a few minutes a small pile of such things lay in the middle of the rooftop, waiting for someone to set it on fire.

"Ready!" Nancy said, looking at the stuff they had collected.

"No, not yet" Daniel said, surprising her. "We must block the door in some way so the animals won't be able to come through!"

"You're right, but with what?" Nancy asked, and started looking around.

"Since the door has a handle, it won't be very difficult. Has anyone noticed if the keys are still in it?"

They all looked at each other. Then they walked quickly to the door. A pair of keys hung on the outside. They wondered why they hadn't seen them, but they didn't spend a long time to think about it. Clara closed the door and turned the key in the lock. For a few seconds they thought they were safe. But they soon remembered what the predators had done with the safety door at Nancy's house! This tin structure on the building's rooftop wouldn't hold them for long, but it was the only thing they had.

"Daniel, come quickly, there are very few vehicles left close to us!"

The boy pulled the lighter out of his pocket and leaned over the rubbish they had gathered. Now, that rubbish was their only hope!

Almost two minutes passed, and the fire was burning fully. The children waved their hands, shouting, but no rescue team approached. It was a sure thing, however, that both the soldiers and the predators had seen them. Now it was simply a matter of who would come first!

Daniel headed towards the edge of the building to see what was going on down in the street. He felt dizzy for a moment, so he moved on all fours. He jumped the guardrail and crawled over the concrete, drawing himself to the edge of the building. Nancy told him to be careful, whatever he was doing. Daniel heard her but he didn't stop.

His head now poked over the side of the roof and he had a view one of Manhattan's wide streets. Darkness made watching difficult but his eyes soon got used to the environment far from the fire and allowed him to see something he wished he hadn't seen!

He didn't have time to count them, but he got the impression that there were more than ten hungry predators entering the building, probably heading for its roof-to them!

"They're coming!" he managed to whisper. The other two didn't hear him. He stood up, forgetting about dizziness and the height at which he stood, and shouted at the top of his voice, "They're coming, I'm telling you. They're here!"

Nancy and Clara froze on hearing his words. Daniel took a deep breath and tried to move on. At that moment, he slipped and found himself in the air!

Nancy screamed; so did Clara. They had lost sight of Daniel!

A few seconds of stillness and intense confusion passed. Then things became clearer when Daniel's voice said, "Will you finally come and get me up from here?"

He was still alive!

Clara ran as fast as she could to where Daniel had fallen. She carefully leaned over and saw the boy hanging from a pipe about half a foot below her. She didn't know what the purpose of that pipe was; she only knew it had saved the life of a child.

"Grab my hand!" she said to the boy hugging the pipe.

"Do you think that's easy?"

"Grab it, Daniel, we haven't got much time!" she shouted and stretched her arm as much as she could.

The boy removed one hand from the pipe and grabbed Clara's hand. A light breeze blew, reminding him that hundreds of feet lay below him. He managed to control his fear.

"They're coming!" he whispered as Clara pulled him up.

A sudden sound, a knock, was enough to scare her Startled, she released the boy's hand. Daniel hung in the air, holding onto the iron pipe with one hand. At the same moment, something slammed against the locked door.

No rescue team was anywhere in sight! The predators had detected them and would do everything possible to get them; after so many days without food, they were ravenous. "Come on, my boy, don't give up!" Clara shouted and stretched out her hand again.

Daniel grasped it. "Don't leave me this time, don't do it! No matter what is waiting for me up there don't let me fall!"

"Come on, get up here," Clara said and gritted her teeth as the boy climbed up by pulling on her arm.

Repeated knocks sounded against the door!

"A helicopter, mum, a helicopter," Nancy shouted behind them.

Clara suddenly used all the strength she had and pulled the pale boy up. She had managed to save him but would the helicopter manage to save them, too?

"Where is it?" she asked, but soon saw the answer herself. It was quite far away but it was getting closer and closer to them!

But the door couldn't hold anymore. The sheets of metal had already bent and the bodies of the predators that were trying to throw it down were visible in the cracks. There were too many, and they were very hungry!

Daniel was sweating. He took deep breaths. He had escaped death from the fall, but he wasn't sure he could escape this time.

When Nancy saw the animals' claws tearing through the metal door, she started screaming.

The helicopter was still far away. It wouldn't arrive in time, and they all knew it.

One last strike that shattered the lock, and the door collapsed onto the rooftop. The predator leaped through.

Clara looked for the helicopter. It would arrive in a minute, but it didn't seem that they would be alive by then.

"Kids!" she whispered, "go to the end of the building and stay there until the helicopter comes!"

"Mum, what do you intend to do?" Nancy asked.

"Just do as I say and don't ask. Go!" Clara said and pushed both kids away. Then she turned to face the predators.

There were ten of them, and they were all looking at her alone. They stood next to one another, forming a front line, imitating the soldiers. They were ready to strike; they were ready!

Clara took a deep breath and approached them.

"Don't, don't do it! " Nancy shouted behind her, but she didn't hear. This was the only way to keep the two children alive, and she was determined to save them.

She moved even closer, resolute, unafraid of facing their cold yellow eyes. They would kill her, that was sure, but that was the only thing they could do to her!

She stopped walking. All ten animals looked at her curiously. Three of them lowered their tails and prepared to attack. But they didn't. They paused to reconsider, to reorganize their attack.

Clara was holding a knife.

She was buying the kids time.

All ten animals started walking around Clara, surrounding her. When the circle closed, leaving their victim no way out, they stopped. Then they all turned and walked in the other direction, trying to confuse her. Clara, holding the knife tightly, turned her eyes to her daughter for the last time.

The helicopter was now hovering above their heads, its occupants watching the situation below. The velociraptors noticed the helicopter that was interrupting their hunting. Some of them growled, but none stopped circling around their victim.

They attacked!

Clara was looking at her daughter; she kept her eyes on Nancy the whole time. Clara fell down with a smile on her lips, a smile few people can obtain.

A rope ladder was thrown out the side of the helicopter. It dropped in front of Daniel and Nancy. Clara wanted to shout at them, "Grab it…, grab it and live by loving each other!" but for some reason, no air would come out of her mouth. She fell into darkness…

Nancy looked in terror at her dying mother. She was screaming, crying; she wanted to go to her. Daniel grasped her by the waist and grabbed the ladder. Their flying savior rose and drew away of the building without waiting for the children to climb up. The long ladder was gradually retracting. The predators didn't notice them.

The helicopter flew between the buildings of Manhattan; cold wind buffeted Daniel and Nancy's agonized faces as they traveled far away from the nightmare. Nancy didn't have the energy to cry anymore. She hung there in Daniel's arms as the ladder swayed in the air, and looked at the spot where her mother had died. The fire illuminated the predators as they had leaned over what had been Clara-mum! But mum had indeed managed to save them, mum was proud of what she had done just before leaving this world.

There will be at least two people who will remember that woman; they will remember Clara and live with the memory of her; they will live with her!

O VARIATION

Very few from the armed forces had remained around Manhattan, on the coast of New Jersey and in the Bronx. Those goal of those who did remain was to delay, but not prevent any attempt by the predators to break out. However, the predators seemed hesitant to attack, perhaps contemplating the return of the forces they had faced a day earlier. They preferred to remain in Manhattan until the scarce food supplies remaining were exhausted. Of course, they didn't have any idea what was waiting for them.

Approximately an hour was left before the deadline and the bombing of New York that, this time, would come from other nations. In the meantime, those around the city donned their special suits, and the American antimissile systems went on alert status.

As a test, a remote-controlled F22 flew in the sky over Manhattan, passing once over the city on the course it would follow during the launch of the O variation. The test flight was fine and the aircraft returned to be equipped with its lethal cargo. Only forty-five minutes remained!

The F22 crossed the sky again, only this time the little tank it carried wasn't empty. Somewhere in the middle of the route, as it was flying slowly along over Central Park, it dropped the tank. Before the little metallic box touched the ground, it exploded high in the air. A pink dust came out of it, creating a small cloud that within seconds had dissipated. The deadly substance was free and ready to take effect on any living thing it encountered.

The people watching the event, safe in their suits, were taken aback by the weapon's form. There were no spectacular explosions, no noise, no overt actions. It was a weapon that killed unnoticeably; it was a "smart" weapon.

The gentle wind spread the O variation all over Manhattan and along the coasts of Long Island as well. The calculations had been accurate enough; the entire area would be covered with just one strike. The effects would show later, on living organisms, on the lab animals that had been placed in four locations at both ends of the island.

One of the lab animals wasn't a monkey as usual, but a living velociraptor. The scientists had already checked the effectiveness of the O variation on a deinonychus in their laboratories, the only one they had managed to capture, and now they wished to see if the animals would die under real conditions, with the release of the O variation outside the laboratory. The results didn't take long to show.

The animal didn't notice the foreign particle that penetrated its organs-it couldn't smell it, it couldn't taste it, but it definitely realized that something was wrong an hour later. It collapsed and began vomiting blood. Its eyes drooped as the animal's organs shut down. Its death wasn't at all quick...

The O variation had provided the miracle; it had killed the enemy but it would also kill humans over the next few days. Of course, the number of deaths it would cause couldn't compare with the damage that would have occurred if the animals had escaped from New York. Mathematics pointed to this choice.

Just how dangerous the poison was that had been used would be kept secret. There would be no warning; a few more people would lose their lives but that didn't matter to the government-they would keep their positions of power! The most tragic aspect of this was that people would one day be grateful to them.

But, for the time being, what was important was the sight unfolding before the astonished eyes of those who were lucky enough-or unlucky enough-to be near that all-powerful biological weapon. The animals dropped dead one after the other, losing consciousness, running in every direction, plunging into the sea, or even tearing at themselves with their sharp claws. They suffered greatly before dying, but no one believed they didn't deserve every second of torment. Those animals had made a very big mistake. They had messed with humankind; they'd tried to mess with their creators!

Everyone in the vicinity wanted to celebrate, but the suits didn't even allow them to shout for their victory. One of the soldiers got carried away, took off his mask and shouted, "Go to hell, you damned creatures!" When he saw his comrades looking at him with sorrow in their eyes, knowing they were looking at someone condemned to die, he put an end to his life within seconds, by putting a bullet in his head. No one tried to stop him.

LIES...

The atmosphere of celebration after the victory in New York, with the extermination of all the predators, spread to the War Room. As far as America was concerned, the threat had been superbly faced and humanity had emerged the winner. By annihilating the predators before the deadline, they would also avoid the nuclear strike threatened by the other countries-a strike that would have had devastating effects on a city like New York, where so many important services were based.

The new president, obviously satisfied, opened the door of the Oval Office and strode in. He looked around, as if seeing it for the first time in his life, and then headed towards his luxurious desk. He sat down and admired himself: the new, albeit un-elected, President of the U.S.A. After he got used to the idea of being the leader of the most powerful nation on earth, he dialed a number on the phone in front of him and waited.

"Yes?" a voice answered.

Foster didn't know why, but it sounded like the man on the other end of the line was shaking. "This is the President. what's going-"

"Mr. President, we have very bad news. I was just about to call you!"

"What do you mean?"

"I'm going to say it quickly; we haven't got much time. The nuclear strike will still happen!"

"God damn it, who told you that?" Foster demanded.

"You can call the government of Argentina, they'll-"

The man didn't have a chance to finish his sentence. The president had already hung up. He quickly dialed the president of Argentina. He wanted to hear this with his own ears, and he would!

"This is President Foster of the United States!" he said before anyone spoke.

The Argentinean president had picked the phone up as if he was expecting Foster to call. "How come you didn't answer my phone calls before now?"

"I ask the questions and you answer!" President Foster said aggressively.

"No problem," the Argentinean president said, "the bomb has already been launched!"

"Why don't you call the nuclear strike off? The predators are all dead!"

"Oh, I'm afraid I can't believe you; I can't believe a man who didn't have the courage to call and warn us before he attacked…"

"I wasn't the President then," Foster protested.

"Listen, Mr. President; my people are thirsty for revenge, and so am I. We can't allow you to bomb everyone you please whenever you feel like it; you're not the leaders of the whole world, god damn it!"

The American President was speechless.

"The ten-megaton hydrogen bomb will strike in the center of Manhattan, and that is something you can no longer prevent!"

"But, we have so many troops around there…"

"Well, you'd better tell them to start running!"

The President cleared his throat anxiously. He had picked the phone with great confidence that he would cow the other president into sub-mission, but it seemed that things had happened the other way around.

"Your missile will never make it to New York!" he said.

"And how will that happen?" the Argentinean demanded. "In God's name, we're fourteen powerful nations; do you even know how many of us have the capability to launch a ten megaton bomb? You don't even know which country it will come from!"

The President harrumphed nervously gain. The other president was right.

"You'd better just let it happen. You have eighteen minutes until detonation. At least we warned you!" the Argentinean said, and hung up.

President Foster didn't put the phone down. He sat holding it to his ear, listening to the dial tone. His career would end far earlier than he had imagined. His dreams were collapsing. And what about the people who were going to die? If he'd cared about them too, he would have never reached the position he was now; he wouldn't even be a member of the government!

But for the time being, he was the president and he was racing the clock. They had to order the missiles for the countermeasure strike out of standby; they had to evacuate the population neighboring New York, they had to warn, to, to, to-all in eighteen minutes! They had known about this worse-case scenario hours ago; it was something that the other countries couldn't have kept secret. They knew about it, but they didn't warn the people living around New York because they were sure of the effectiveness of the O variation, and assumed the credibility of the other countries' word. The mistake would be all theirs, not the other fourteen countries. Now the clock was counting down again, but this time for them. Now they realized what they had done!

NUCLEAR DISASTER

Foster stood in front of a giant electronic map displaying four objects of unidentified nature flying over the Atlantic Ocean from Europe. They were heading toward New York. Six more had left at a different moment from Argentina, also with New York as the target. All the missiles would arrive at the same time. The United States had ten very fast missiles to deal with, one of which carried a lethal payload. No matter how hard they tried, they would never disable all of ten of them in time.

"Where do you believe the nuclear warhead will come from?" the president asked the Secretary of Defense.

"In my opinion, from Argentina. But there's nothing to stop them from having foreseen my prediction and taking the necessary measures."

"Very well. I want you to concentrate all your efforts on the four missiles from Europe; the hydrogen bomb must be amongst those."

"We've already sent air missions but it won't be at all easy...You know; I believe we should let this bomb strike."

The President looked at him, horrified. "What did you say?"

"Think about it; the casualties would be very few. Moreover, even if we ward off this attack, nothing can stop them from launching another. We are being led to a world war, sir; someone has to give way and that someone must be us!"

"What you're saying is very correct, but have you considered what the citizens of this country would then say?" Foster asked. "They would rise against us and they would be absolutely right to do so! Do you prefer civil war to world war?"

"I can't have any opinion when we're being threatened with civil war."

"But we're the ones who are being called on to decide and we will decide what's best for us," the president declared. "If that takes us to a third world war then let it be so!"

For the first time, the Secretary of Defense was seeing the real personality of the former vice-president. He regretted voting for the man now, but there was nothing he could do to take it back. He was forced to accept the president's wishes and handle whatever would follow.

"How much time before our aircraft intercept the missiles over the Atlantic?" the president asked.

"Fifty seconds to visual contact," an officer monitoring the four intercept aircraft announced. "Whatever is going to happen will happen in the next ten minutes."

The aircraft, each armed with its own missiles, flew over the four missiles flying toward New York. Then they turned and approached them from behind.

The four remote-controlled missiles began drawing away from each other, thus forcing the aircraft formation to split. No more than four minutes had passed before the American weapons targeted the propulsion systems of the nuclear warheads. They would shoot them down over the Atlantic Ocean, where it didn't matter if there was an explosion or not. A big tidal wave would be better than an annihilating nuclear wave!

Three of the aircraft armed their missiles, which were based on the latest American technology and had a likelihood of only three percent of missing their target once they were launched. There was nothing more left to do but press a button, and so it happened.

Now, four possible nuclear missiles, four aircraft and the three smaller American counter-missiles traveled through the sky. Three, and not four!

One of the four aircraft reported its systems jammed. There was no radar image, and communication was very soon cut off, as well as control of the plane. The pilot managed to eject before his aircraft hurtled into the ocean waves, and exploded into a thousand pieces.

The other three missiles that had been launched successfully reached their targets. The chill morning air over the ocean was filled with explosions that seemed like fireworks to watching Americans. The explosions were extremely bright and the flames were clearly visible even in the light of the dawning sun. But unfortunately, darkness still prevailed in the United States....

There were still seven missiles left and the government believed they knew which one carried the hydrogen bomb-the only missile still flying from Europe to New York, the only one of the four missiles that had been equipped with anti-aircraft systems to protect its valuable load.

The three remaining aircraft that had been sent to intercept entered safe operation mode, a technology that prevented the blocking of their systems by a nuclear missile's anti-aircraft system, and approached the fourth and last missile. All three of them fired two missiles each, without approaching further than the necessary distance. Nothing seemed to go wrong. At least, not in the beginning!

At first, one of the three aircraft went down; the other two managed to pull away. Then the missile increased speed, prolonging very much the time the other six, smaller but faster missiles would take to reach it. Everyone was astonished.

"Approach again and fire all the missiles you've got left!" came the order from the radio.

"Okay, message received!" the pilots of both aircraft acknowledged, and gained speed. As they closed, they saw the six missiles they had fired blowing up in mid-air without anything touching them. It was as if the nuclear missile had ordered their electronic circuits to explode on the spot. Not even the Americans had such technology; at least, not that they had made public knowledge.

One of the two aircraft began losing altitude, its systems paralyzed; the pilot ejected. Now there was only one aircraft left.

The pilot decreased speed at once, knowing that he would face the same fate as his partners if he kept on. He knew very well that he was the last hope of the United States. If he didn't destroy that missile, then no one would!

He drew far from the missile. Then, he spoke over his radio. "Is there any way to keep the jet engine functional while the electronic systems are off?"

"There is, but the aircraft will become very unsteady, it will be very difficult!" was the answer. "Tell me how," he demanded, defying danger.

"First approach the missile with the systems on because otherwise you won't make it."

The pilot set both engines at full. "I'll be next to the missile in thirty seconds," he said.

"Very well." Mission control gave him instructions on what to press on his board. The plan was very simple, but it was the only one they had.

Reaching the missile, the pilot unhesitatingly shut down all electronic systems; the engines were the only thing still on. The aircraft made a strange sound but it continued to fly, with a few bumps, drawing closer and closer to the missile without going down like the other three had.

He could see its tail! He was now right behind the missile, but the aircraft's instability was growing very dangerous. He had to hurry.

In seconds, he restored all electronic systems and fired all the missiles he had left. The nuclear missile exploded.

Flaming pieces of the missile flew in every direction. The bomb had been defused, but the radioactive materials had been set free. The pilot of the aircraft didn't manage to gain altitude before his plane hit one of the pieces of the missile and he was burned together with his plane.

On the other side of the ocean, the members of the American government were clapping at his heroism. But even further south, in Argentina, operations continued as though nothing had ended. The six missiles flying from there to New York were continuing their course and would reach their target in a few minutes.

The hydrogen bomb was still in the air, and the American government didn't know it!

"Mr. President," someone in the War Room asked, "why do the other six missiles coming from Argentina continue flying if they aren't carrying the hydrogen bomb?"

"They're playing with our nerves. We found the missile carrying it and we stopped it," Foster said and laughed derisively. "Those countries will learn that no one can mess with the United States!"

At the same moment, a red circle was forming on their map, above New York.

"Mr. President..."

"What is it now?"

A rumble, like an earthquake shook the building.

"I think you must see this," the Secretary of Defense said and pointed over the president's shoulder at the map.

The red circle was growing bigger, swallowing Long Island and Brooklyn, and many more areas. One of the six Argentinean bombs had gone off!

THE ANALYSIS

The buildings of Manhattan had been wiped from the face of the earth. A great part of the land Manhattan had stood on had been buried under the ocean, while the tidal wave raised covered several miles of Long Island, Brooklyn and the surrounding areas. The effect, aside from the water that devoured New York, was the same as that incurred by the bomb that had struck Buenos Aires. The destruction was equal.

But this time, the U.S. government didn't celebrate at all. The account of the dead, the destruction, but above all, the turmoil that would develop around them brought despair. They had paid in kind.

The new president of the United States considered how quickly that fact would terminate his ambitious career. For a moment, he wanted to kill all the members of the government of Argentina. Such rage could be very dangerous in a time of great decision, like this one.

"At least we're absolutely sure that the O variation has been neutralized," the Secretary of Defense said, seeming unsurprised by the strike against New York.

"Yes" the president said, "that's something." He stepped to the electronic map and took a close look at the red dot. From this close, the degree of destruction, the full scope of all those areas rendered useless for decades, seemed much clearer!

"Will the radioactivity affect us here, in Washington?" he asked without taking his eyes from the map.

"No, Mr. President, the wind is still blowing from the south."

"Mr. President, they want you on the phone," someone said from the back of the room. "It's about the analysis of the data from the farm, I think; that's what they said."

"Put them through on line twenty-six," Foster said and picked up the phone next to him.

"This is the President."

"Mr. President, I think we've found it!"

"Found what?"

"The solution to our problem, of course!"

The President held his head. "If only you had done that half an hour ago, just half an hour earlier…"

"Why, what happened?" the caller asked.

"We would have been able to blackmail the other countries by telling them we have the solution! But now…"

"Blackmail them?"

"You don't know what has happened; you will soon find out. Tell me now, what is the solution?" Foster asked.

"Look, the entire development process was in the records you gave us!"

"I know, go on," Foster prompted.

"Looking through them, we came across a file about safety measures. It was very difficult to understand but we eventually did it."

"Did what?"

"Well, whoever designed those things-about three species of dinosaurs-"

"What, what, three species?" The president was shocked. They'd only encountered two species.

"Oh, don't worry; one of the three probably didn't survive to escape from the farm," the scientist assured him.

Clive had never talked to them about a third species, Foster thought. It seemed Clive had taken many secrets with him.

"So, as I was saying, the man who developed them made sure to take some security measures. You'd be surprised at what those measures are!"

"Some virus, I suppose..."

"It is indeed a virus, unknown up to now, that leads the animal to cannibalism!"

"What did you say?" Foster sputtered.

"Cannibalism, sir. In other words, it alters their instincts, forcing them to eat one another. And you know what the best thing is? It doesn't affect humans or other life forms at all; it's harmless to us!"

The president was thunderstruck. He considered how many lives would have been saved if they had waited for this phone call, if they had waited for just ten hours. The predators had been exterminated on the American continent, but their numbers were still growing in Asia and Australia. If that virus did indeed do what it promised to do, he, Foster, would be heralded as the savior of the world!

"Do you have any of the virus ready? I mean, can we test it on living predators?"

"We have already produced the virus according to the instructions and it is probably what it should be. You know; it wasn't easy to understand what was written in those old records."

"Very well! Send us the formula, so we can cultivate the virus here, too!"

"We've already e-mailed it," the scientist said. "You'll receive it on Computer Thirteen."

"Okay. I want you to stay in direct contact with my scientists!" Foster instructed him.

"Consider it done. Although I don't think they'll have any difficulty. The virus is very easily produced as long as you know what to use. Ah, I have a question. Should we continue with the analysis of the data?"

"Of course you should," Foster said without thinking. "I have to go now." He hung up the phone, then ordered the computer operators to receive the e-mail.

In a short time, the news had spread everywhere. The U.S.A. had a weapon that could release the world from the threat of the predators! The government of Australia, almost paralyzed by the disaster, eagerly asked for the virus without delay. Asia reported that two more cities had been conquered by the velociraptors. Whatever was to happen, would have to happen quickly!

THE TEST!

The virus, with the code name "red.Dc-1", had been produced. The only thing left before its release into earth atmosphere over the stricken areas was to check its effectiveness. A test on live predators in a specially reinforced chamber was arranged. Every person of any importance was there to observe.

Two velociraptors behaved as though they were rabid. They hit the unbreakable glass and scratch at the doors, trying to get out of the small enclosure. All the members of the government stood on the other side, watching the predators' torment as they tried to get out. Some couldn't stand the loud screams of the animals and, horrified to see the creatures in front of them, they fainted. Finally, only sixteen important people remained in the room to witness what happened.

A scientist in a white uniform entered the observation area and spoke to the observers. "Now we will release the virus. For this small area a microgram is enough; for the outside, we will need many kilograms."

He pressed a switch. Nothing seemed to change in the room. No white gas come out of the vents as many expected. Whatever had been released was invisible, but lethal-at least, for the predators.

The animals froze, as if thinking, as if they were reconsidering the situation. Some likened the reaction to a computer, when you load a new program into it. Then the creatures moved.

They weren't trying to get out anymore. It was obvious that one felt threatened by the presence of the other. They started circling, staring one another in the eyes. They were enemies!

A smile split the president's face. Then everyone shut their eyes as a stream of blood splattered from one end of the window to the other. One of them had attacked the other!

Strange sounds came from the predator's mouth before it died.

The man in white whispered, "Now this is the most crucial point!"

The other predator, which had suffered nothing more than a small cut, looked at the blood of its companion with bleary eyes. After a while it grew more courageous. It bent and started tearing at the flesh of its own species and swallowing large pieces of it.

"That was it!" the scientist shouted, astonished. "Now, please watch what's going to happen if we place prey of a different species in the chamber."

A small door in the wall of the chamber opened and a monkey was pushed through. The door closed immediately behind it, leaving it exposed to the velociraptor.

The predator raised its head, looking at the other animal in curiosity. The blood of the other velociraptor dripped from its jaws.

The small monkey started screaming and running up and down. The predator followed its movements with an aggressive look. Once it was ensured that it wasn't in any danger from the strange, small animal, it returned to its victim, continuing to eat. Everything had turned out as hoped!

"Congratulations!" the president said and shook the hand of the scientist. "You've just saved the world!"

THE END OF OUR END!

The time had come, the moment that all people on the earth had been expecting for days. The predators had been completely exterminated in America, but not in Asia. There, the underdeveloped countries were powerless to face the threat and were simply waiting for a miracle, help from the sky to save them. Who could expect that that miracle would indeed happen and that it would come from the sky!

Twenty helicopters and six planes, armed with the new antidote of humanity, the red.DC-1, flew over the devastated areas of Australia and Eastern Asia. They carried the hope of the entire world: a deadly virus that promised to save the humans that were left by turning the predators on themselves.

No government denied permission for the release of the virus in its airspace. One way or the other, they didn't have any choice. The aircraft and helicopters circled above the spot where they would leave their payload, waiting for the order.

The President of the United States took the microphone and said, "Release it! "

The aircraft released from their tanks a red fluid that immediately vaporized. After a while it wasn't visible at all, but it still existed, dispersed in the air, ready to infect all its living targets. The red.DC-1 was in the air breathed by humans.

No more than two minutes passed before the virus struck its victims. The predators killed each other, attacking their own nests, putting their own broods to death. The same creatures that, if they had merely seen a human, that person was as good as dead, were now ignoring people as if their brains had been totally altered. They were still as deadly, but this time their aggression was to humanity's advantage.

Within a day, 97% of the predators had killed each other without any human having to lift a finger. Some predators took refuge in forests but they were condemned to die there, now biologically programmed to feed only on the meat of their own species, which was something they couldn't find anymore. The damage to their brains was permanent.

Humanity celebrated that day! People celebrated the undeniable victory; the horrible death suffered by the enemy. But above all, people were celebrating for their lives, which they had managed to preserve while at the same time millions of others died next to them. Those ones, the dead, were unable to celebrate.

That day, people were happy and united. At such moments, even the worst enemies shook hands, forgot their hatred and realized something that had eluded them for so long. It took a common threat to make all the great nations to fight against each other, and it took that same threat to unite all the smaller nations of the world and make them more powerful than the greatest of the great!

Argentina congratulated the U.S.A. despite the fact that two dead cities separated them. The new president made plans for the future, as he deserved. The whole world wept with happiness over the dead bodies of the predators, those creatures that, without being aware of it, had caused so much good to come in the civilization named humanity. The predators made humans realize that they are something more than merely a civilization.

HISTORY'S PAGES...

DISCLOSURES!

One day after the most beautiful day of mankind, as the research into the records of the farm continued, the scientists were rewarded much more than expected. This time the experts didn't call the White House, but instead the media, making public terrible truths that, had they been in the hands of the government, would have been concealed forever. The magazines had something to write about for an entire month.

What had managed to unite all the people on earth, that mistake that turned into a tragedy and then a salvation, was a human mistake! The dead President Bennett Clive had known all about the case; this revelation was based on proof that had come from the offices of the biotechnological company NeoGene. Equally involved was the Secretary of Defense, who was arrested and would probably be executed by lethal injection.

Those two people concealed the development of the living weapons to benefit the U.S.A. of course, but it turned out to be disastrous for themselves and for the rest of the world as well. International treaties were violated and the result was several million dead people.

The basic goal of the program that was so deceptively named "the farm" was the development of deadly organisms with high intelligence. Time and money weren't to be wasted, so they avoided the construction of a whole organism from the beginning. Therefore, they worked from creatures that had already lived in the past and had a remarkable predatory record. Three dinosaur species were judged appropriate: velociraptors, deinonychuses, and utahraptors. The last model never entered the production process and thus didn't have the chance to escape the farm.

The information that led to the construction of the modern models was found in the "worthless DNA" of birds and reptiles-the genetic remains of previous species like dinosaurs. After the selection of the physical model and its optimization they came up against the issue of intelligence. The decision they reached on that question played the greatest part in the effectiveness of the new organism. They decided to use parts of the DNA of a *human* cell, the kind of cell that determines intellectual development and function. Thus, they created a perfect species!

The cleverness of the predators proved to have originated from our own. Though far from perfect, it proved enough for the creatures to be capable of planning and reaching a substandard level of communication. They chose to take advantage of their mental capabilities by inventing horrible methods of putting the enemy to death, and similar atrocities. Although nothing was absolutely confirmed, experts claimed that the enemy did not develop that trait on its own; it was introduced with the nucleotide chains of the human DNA.

In other words, they were saying that our brain was sick enough that the dinosaurs, with the physical weapons they possessed, could adopt such horrible execution methods. The satisfaction someone experiences when watching a victim crawl and plead for mercy is an exclusively human privilege.

All that time, humanity was fighting against itself! Maybe that's why we nearly lost; maybe that's why we shuddered at every action performed by those animals. In a roundabout way, humans murdered the people who died by the predators' attacks; we were their executioners!

THE CHILDREN

Nancy and Daniel were left open-mouthed with shock when they heard that the city they had escaped from a while earlier had turned into dust. Nancy cried once more for her mother, since it was now completely pointless to hold any hope for her survival. Daniel stayed close to her, since she had nowhere to go. The state would care for them both. They were considered heroes, while their story was told all over the world.

A few days later, Daniel found his father, who was a sailor and had been at sea during the destruction. His father had thought Daniel dead and had already mourned for his child, until a day came when he saw Daniel's face in the newspaper under the headline *Three Days in Hell!* After that, he did everything possible to get to Washington, where Daniel was.

Nancy didn't have many relatives she could count on anymore. She would have been taken to an orphanage, but when the boy's father heard that her mother had given her life to save Daniel and Nancy, he didn't hesitate to adopt her.

The two children grew up like brother and sister, turning their love into affection for one another of the same blood.

They lived together happily on one of the tropical islands of the Atlantic, far away from technology and modern comforts and far closer to life.

Clara lived as long as each of the children did, in the memories of those she had saved. Her face was engraved in the minds of Nancy and Daniel forever. At least two people in the entire world had shed a tear for her sake in one of the oceans; for the sake of an important, courageous woman who knew what self-sacrifice and love meant.

The human mind is, after all, worthy of its existence, if only so that it remembers and recollects...

CLIVE

He remembered the dream; he remembered the dreams he'd had as a child. It had nothing to do with what he was now living. He remembered his first love and then, then he remembered the hydrogen bomb, the great explosion! Suddenly, he didn't want to remember anything anymore.

The next day the press wrote about the death of the President of the United States, but no one mourned for him, no one in the entire world.

However, the press doesn't always say the truth, perhaps because they often don't know the truth. This was the case in the story of the president's suicide, a well-constructed fable created by one person in the world, and that person was the hero of the story himself, Clive.

He had never died; he had never put a bullet in his head. He was far too much of a coward to kill himself, but man enough to kill millions of others. He wasn't the only one on this planet like that; it's full of them.

He lived many more years, on some remote island that no one ever set foot on, trying to forget. The saltiness of the sea wore at him; that and his beard made him unrecognizable. He called on some people to provide him with the necessities for his survival from time to time, but none of them ever suspected who he was.

As far as the supposed suicide was concerned, it was a very well-staged ruse in which a human copy of the president, a clone that he himself had raised in a tube unbeknownst to anyone else, was killed instead of Clive himself.

However, somewhere near the end of his natural lifespan, Clive didn't escape suicide. He willingly plunged from a tall cliff. He was a man completely different from the man he'd been before; still a coward, but also a man who regretted his past deeds. He had found the courage; he was ready to go.

The punishment that had been inflicted on him prior to his death was loneliness, nightmares, and remorse; all of which eventually pushed him over the edge of the cliff into the sea.

His body was lost in the ocean waves, where he actually died. As for the man that most people in the world hated for the wrongs he had caused, no, that man wasn't the Clive that died in the Atlantic waters. That man had died that day in the president's office: a dead conscience, a masked personality, and a shell of a body covering what everyone refused to see.

GOVERNMENT

Every politician but the Secretary of Defense managed to convince the people that they had done the best they could and that they were the ones who managed to save the world after all. The new president remained in office for many years by constantly condemning the former President Clive and repeatedly reminding them that he, not Clive, had given the order for the use of the red.DC-1.

The politicians lived on by sucking the blood of the people, without feeling any remorse for the suffering they had induced with their nuclear attacks. They lived on, conscienceless, destroying their lives and the lives of others. They, the real predators of today's society, felt not the slightest twinge of remorse, even though they deserved the worst nightmares in the world. They'd never shed a real tear in their lives; how could they know about life?

But, those people should indeed feel sorry for themselves! Because as they were passing away, wondering what they had done in those ruined lives of theirs, at that moment when there can be no lies, they had no answer to give.

Barry, Clara and so many millions of people had so much to say, but there was nothing they could say. In the end, the politicians died one after the other, having thousands of people around them that believed in them, followed them, but never ever loved them.

Epilogue

That crucial moment for mankind had passed and mankind was still alive, whether that life was deserved or not. But the story of humanity needed a different end; it needed an end! Words that the poem itself whispers, our history...
...then the legs bent
they didn't stand the weight
and...
like a wind that constantly blows
like a sun that rises
like the star that stands up there
like the dream that ceases breathing
no one felt sorry for it
no one said what a pity
a love seized it
and it was lost in the wave

The end, however, didn't come-at least, not at this stage of our story, when the first hydrogen bomb went off above Buenos Aires "like a wind that constantly blows, like a sun that rises..."
The end hadn't come yet but it would soon come, nothing could stop it. Behind every important decision we have made always lies an end,

even if it has never revealed itself. Important decisions, however, are made every day...

And the poem was not mistaken; it did not even have one wrong verse, in the centuries of human history. But the poem wanted humanity to be lost, to be buried under its greed, its great dreams. The poem said that something like that was going to happen very soon and that no one would be able to stop it. That's what it was saying...

But no! No, as long as humans are the only poets of this world; no, as long as humans can write the verses of history themselves; no, as long as humans can write verses...

The End?